“I want you, Renée Walker. I want you so bad I can’t sleep.”

“I want you too,” she moaned.

Daniel ran his hand down her back, remembering the sensitive spot along her spine. She breathed in deeply, her body tense with her need.

“Come,” Daniel said. “I want to make love to you right here on the sand.”

They moved toward the line of tall palm trees, stopping when they reached the shadows where no one could see them. She rested her back against one of the trees and he looked down at her, only to see that her eyes were closed.

“Look at me, Renée. I want you to look at me,” he said, his voice husky with desire.

She complied, her eyes bright lights in [illegible] darkness.

“I love to feel your eyes on me, k[illegible] you want me just as much as I w[illegible]

“Are you going to sto[illegible] asked.

“Your wish is my [illegible] and he lowered his head, [illegible] a searing kiss.

Books by Wayne Jordan

Kimani Romance

Embracing the Moonlight
One Gentle Knight
To Love a Knight
Always a Knight
Midnight Kisses

WAYNE JORDAN

For as long as he can remember, Wayne Jordan loved reading, but he also enjoyed creating his own make-believe worlds. This love for reading and writing continued and in November 2005 his first book, *Capture the Sunrise,* was published by BET Books.

Wayne has always been an advocate for romance, especially African-American romance. In 1999 he founded www.romanceincolor.com, a Web site which focuses on African-American romance and its authors.

Wayne is a high school teacher and a graduate of the University of the West Indies. He holds a B.A. in Literature and Linguistics and an M.A. in Applied Linguistics. He lives on the beautiful tropical island of Barbados, which, with its white sands and golden sunshine, is the perfect setting for the romance stories he loves to create.

Midnight KISSES

WAYNE JORDAN

To those who have lost their faith and need healing… you need only look to the *One* who gives life and love.

To my editor, Kelli Martin, who encouraged me to dig beneath the surface and tap into that hidden sensitivity inside me and, in the process, helped me to become a much better writer.

Recycling programs for this product may not exist in your area.

ISBN-13: 978-0-373-86182-8

MIDNIGHT KISSES

www.kimanipress.com

Printed in U.S.A.

Dear Reader,

I hope you enjoy *Midnight Kisses,* Daniel Buchanan's story. Writing this book was a truly emotional experience.

In *Embracing the Moonlight* readers discovered that Daniel had lost his wife and daughter. But I couldn't write this story immediately. I needed to give Daniel some time to heal before he could resolve his issues with his faith and his feelings toward relationships. Of course, love plays a significant part in his journey toward healing. I hope I've succeeded and that you are touched by Daniel and Renée's story.

After *Midnight Kisses* I plan to return to characters who keep begging me to write their stories. The series I am currently working on is tentatively titled Dark, Sexy, Cool and features secondary characters from The Knight Trilogy. *Tempted by the Doctor* is Troy Whitehall's story and is scheduled to be released in July 2011. George's and Jared's stories will follow in 2012.

I love hearing from my readers, so please feel free to contact me at authorwj@caribsurf.com.

Thanks for your continued support.

Wayne

Prologue

Thanksgiving Night

The succulent odor of baked turkey and cranberry sauce wafted through the air from the apartment below, bringing memories of a time when his life had been perfect. Daniel Buchanan stood on the balcony looking out at the Chicago skyline.

He'd been in Chicago for almost six months now, and he was finally beginning to feel settled. For a year, he had traveled all over the U.S. before finally settling in Chicago, his anger at God and at the world hindering his healing. He had still not found the peace of mind he'd been searching for. Now he was closer to home, his restlessness tempered by a need to be close to the familiar.

A vivid image of his youth in Oak Park flashed in his mind. He missed his childhood. Those were the happy days, when he and his brothers had raced with the wind and reached for the skies.

The slow hands of time had changed things, and not all for the better. At first life had seemed perfect. After college he'd accepted an assignment at a church in Brooklyn, married the ideal wife…and then his perfect world had crumbled. He'd lost his wife and child. He'd lost everything. He'd run away.

But he was tired of running. Today was another step on his road to healing. He'd secured a good job and he was ready to face the memories that haunted him. Today, he wanted to focus on the present. He needed to bury the past were it belonged.

A star flashed across the sky drawing him from his memories.

Thanksgiving—he had nothing to be thankful for. He'd lost all that he had. His beautiful wife and the daughter he would never see or hold in his arms.

The familiar rage threatened to resurface but he suppressed it, willing it under control. There was no longer time for anger. He'd dealt with his feelings and had come to an acceptance that his life had changed and he had to stop running; that nothing he did would bring them back.

Unfortunately, it was in these silent hours that the loneliness almost seemed to drown him. He would not cry. He'd already cried enough for his loss. Tonight, he'd celebrate the fact that he was still alive; that he had survived.

In the distant sky a bright star pitched across the wide expanse, and he smiled for the first time in months. Maybe someday he'd find a reason to wish upon a star. Maybe someday, he'd find happiness again.

Renée Walker slammed the door behind her, wondering for the umpteenth why she didn't give up.

Tonight had been a disaster.

As she slipped from the slinky red dress, which clung to her every curve, she wondered what she'd done wrong to deserve a night like the one she'd just faced. After tonight, she had all intentions of swearing off men altogether. Hadn't being jilted at the altar taught her anything?

Last week, her mother, forever the matchmaker, had invited her for dinner at the house. Renée had agreed to attend because it was Thanksgiving and her mother had wanted her to meet Jean, an old school friend. Little did Renée know that the friend's egotistical, pompous son, Leonard, would also be in attendance!

When Renée had finally decided she couldn't deal with his subtle groping or his need to expound his virtues, she had excused herself, claiming a headache. She considered it a close call.

Despite her first impression at dinner, she had still agreed to go out with Leonard. She had done it as a favor to her mom and Jean.

After tedious dinner conversation, she'd declined dessert and called the night short.

The insult came after listening to him boast about his sexual prowess. He'd had the gall to assume that he would spend the night at her apartment…and had been surprised when she had not invited him in.

The exchange between the two of them had not been pleasant and he'd left with a final, "No wonder your fiancé dumped you. You're one cold bitch."

Now, she moved slowly to her bedroom, stopping briefly to put in a CD, and raise the volume on her home theater system.

She stood on the balcony outside her bedroom. The city of Chicago stretched out before her. Midnight—her favorite time of night. The time of magic and kisses… and possibilities. She needed a little magic in her life.

In the dull sky, a star hurled to earth and then disappeared.

Renée wondered if there was some man out there for her. She ached for love, for the kind of happiness her parents had. She hoped one day she would find a good man who'd kiss her until she swooned.

When another star flashed across the sky, she made a wish.

"Help me," she whispered into the night. "Help me find true love."

Chapter 1

Two years later

Daniel Buchanan closed the door behind him and exited the building where he spent most of his waking hours. He'd planned to leave hours ago. Now, in the still hours of early Saturday morning, he was finally heading home.

Outside, the chill of the approaching autumn reminded him that he should have put on his coat. He walked down the steps quickly, heading directly for the only car that remained in the parking lot.

He started the car before he reached it, hoping that the interior would be a bit warm by the time he crossed the forty or so feet to get inside. When he reached the car, he immediately stepped inside, closed the door and pulled out of his reserved spot.

A few minutes later, the cool, mellow croon of the late Luther Vandross serenaded him as he cruised along the almost deserted streets. Thirty minutes and he'd be at the apartment.

The next two days were his days off and he had all intentions of spending them doing nothing but reading and watching a movie or two. Jerome, the teenager he mentored, was in Washington, D.C., on a school tour, so his Saturday would be free. But he missed him. He'd grown so accustomed to the boy being a part of his life that having a weekend schedule that didn't include Jerome left him feeling strange and somewhat empty. He did have some cleaning and laundry to do, so he'd take care of those chores first. After that, he would rest.

He didn't sleep much. Even after three years, sleep came in spits and spurts.

When Daniel neared his building, he instinctively reduced speed. The empty apartment didn't appeal to him, but he knew he had no choice. Nothing could replace the home he'd built with his wife, Lorraine.

After the funeral, he'd sold the house he and Lorraine had built together. For a year, he'd roamed around the U.S., only to settle in Chicago, closer to his boyhood home in Oak Park.

It was now September, a little more than two years since he'd arrived in Chicago, and though he enjoyed his job, he still felt no sense of belonging.

Sometimes in the stillness of the empty house he

heard Lorraine's voice. Sometimes he heard her whisper his name. His wife.

Even after almost three years, he still considered her his wife. Late wife was more like it. But saying the words, as he did now, made him ache with an intensity he thought would have diminished over time.

He had just turned onto the street where he lived when he caught a glimpse of someone being dragged into the alley just ahead. Then he heard a cry, sharp and filled with fear.

He stopped when he reached the alley, turning to point his car inward. The lights startled them both. A man and woman were struggling.

As Daniel rushed from the car, the man pushed the woman away, and Daniel saw her head connect with the wall before she crumpled to the ground.

The man scowled at him, turned and raced down the alley.

Instinctively, Daniel reached for his cell phone, aware that several other cars had stopped, as well.

Dialing 911, he quickly informed them of the problem, only hanging up when they told him that help was on the way.

He looked down at the woman on the ground. No, not a woman, she was just a girl. She couldn't be more than sixteen.

He knelt, taking his jacket off, noticing the blueness of her skin and the frailness of her body. She was all skin and bones beneath the flimsy dress she wore. Blood flowed from a wound on her head.

In the distance, he heard the sirens. Good, help was on the way.

He searched for her pulse. It was weak but steady. She'd be okay, he hoped.

Daniel looked at the innocent face and wondered what a young girl would be doing out so late. He experienced a familiar sadness when the answer dawned on him.

Behind him, the ambulance stopped and he became aware of the people who had gathered at the entrance to the alley. A voice demanded that they clear the way.

He stood, making room for the paramedics. He watched them closely, intent on discovering whether the girl would be all right or not.

For some reason, when he looked at her face, he remembered the times he had dealt with teenagers… runaways. In his ministry, working with teenagers had been his calling. And now, at The Hope Center, his tasks surrounded the teenagers who needed him the most.

Strange that at this precise moment his past would rear its head. He tried not to think of his life in Brooklyn. Most other nights at home, though he could not sleep, he'd almost perfected the ability to keep the images from his past just where they belonged…in the past. Except on the rare occasions when he heard those whispers in the night.

Daniel watched as the paramedics placed the girl on a stretcher and lifted her into the ambulance. Moments later the ambulance sped away, its blue lights flashing, its siren screeching in the quiet of the early morning.

He moved quickly to his car, started it and headed in the direction of the fading sirens.

Vincent Memorial, the hospital where the girl was being taken, was only about ten minutes away.

His hands trembled on the steering wheel.

He'd didn't particularly want to go to the hospital, but he knew that he finally had to confront his demons.

Renée sipped from the glass of lemonade, which had long lost its chill. She forced the drink down, knowing that she would more than likely not get anything else in her stomach before she reached her home in a few hours.

It was after midnight and she was tired; the night had been a long one. Her job as one of four social workers on staff at the hospital was not easy, but she loved the work she did. However, moments like these always left her with a sense of loss.

The telephone's strident ring pulled her from her musings.

"Renée," the voice of Cheryl Archer, her best friend and the hospital administrator on duty, greeted her, "we need you to come down to emergency immediately."

When the line disconnected, Renée quickly dropped what she was doing and headed to the Emergency Room. She dreaded these calls. She prayed that she did not have to deal with death again.

Downstairs, Cheryl greeted her with a tired smile. "I can see that you're feeling just like I am. Four more hours and we'll be on our way home but duty calls. We admitted a young girl an hour ago. She's awake, but we can't get any information out of her."

"A runaway?" Renée asked.

"Looks that way. I'm not even sure if she's in any condition to tell us anything at the moment. She is conscious right now, but I'm not sure how long that will last. She took a hard blow to her head. Maybe you can see what you can find out." She touched Renée's hand. "I know today wasn't easy for you."

"It's fine. It's my job."

"I know, Ms. Dedicated," Cheryl said, forcing a pained smile.

"Oh, so I'm the dedicated one. And here I was thinking that honor was yours. At least I leave the hospital on my off days. When is the last time you went home?"

When her friend did not respond, Renée knew she'd struck a nerve.

"Cheryl, when is the last time you went home?" Renée asked again.

Her friend hesitated before she answered.

"Four days. But you know I have a bed I can use," Cheryl answered before Renée could object. "I didn't have a reason to go home. Julian is away on business. And we were dealing with that little boy's case. We had to move fast. By the way, the police have arrested his mother's boyfriend."

"I know. I'm glad they finally caught the bastard," Renée replied. "Let me go visit with Jane Doe and see if I have some success."

"I'll wait out here until you're done."

Renée turned from her friend and entered the examining room.

When she entered, the girl looked up.

A pretty girl despite the bruises, Renée observed. And scared, too, though she tried to hide it with a brave face.

"Hi," Renée said softly.

The girl relaxed noticeably, but did not reply.

"I'm Renée. What's your name?"

Again, no answer, only a silent stare. Her distrust was evident.

"Okay, you don't have to tell me. Can we call your parents? Relatives?"

"I don't have any," the girl finally said, averting her eyes. "Where's the man?" she asked. Her gaze darted to the door as if she expected him to appear.

"The man?" Renée replied. "The man who attacked you?"

"No, the one who saved me."

"I don't know. I'll have to ask."

"I want to tell him thank you."

"Okay, I will see if I can find him. Now, tell me something about yourself. What's your name?"

"Don't want to talk. My head hurts." The girl turned her head and closed her eyes.

Renée looked down at her. She knew she would get nothing more from the girl, not tonight. Maybe tomorrow she'd be luckier. If she could find the mysterious man who'd rescued her, maybe then she'd talk.

Turning to leave the room, Renée stopped when she heard a soft whisper.

She hadn't heard properly, but it sounded as if the patient had whispered the word *Angel.*

* * *

Daniel felt his stomach churn. He hated the antiseptic odor of the hospital. A wave of nausea slowed his steps. He stopped, breathed in deeply and forced himself to continue.

The corridor echoed with the firm staccato of his footsteps on the spotless white tiles. He stifled the overwhelming urge to tiptoe, knowing that he was being ridiculous.

Why couldn't hospitals have some color? Maybe red or yellow for cheer. The dull gray reminded him of a night he didn't want to remember. Daniel forced the memories from his mind.

He'd reached the end of the corridor. The lights shone brighter here. Flowers, vivid red and yellow, languished in tiny vases on tables in the waiting area to the left of the nurses' station. He headed to the nurse on duty, nodding politely at those in close proximity, aware of the eyes that smiled back at him, and those that lingered.

He never ceased to be amazed that women found him attractive. He, an ordained minister. Well, he was no longer of that vocation, but it still caused him discomfort when women stared at him so boldly. For that reason alone, he missed his collar.

His last embarrassment had taken place just a few days ago at the Center. One of the assistants had left him a gift, a bottle of his favorite cologne. She was almost fifteen years his junior, but he'd noticed the way her eyes seem to devour him. He could not imagine what a girl of her age could find appealing about him.

That night, he'd stared long and hard at himself in

the mirror, realizing that he didn't look quite bad for his age. His brothers were known for their good looks—and he did look a lot like them. He had that tall, lithe but well-toned frame and amber eyes that women seemed to love.

The nurse cleared her throat, drawing him for his momentary lapse.

"I've come to get some information about the young lady that was just brought in?" he said quickly

"We did just admit a few young girls, sir. Can you be a bit more specific?"

"Sorry, the young lady who was beaten up?" he replied.

"Are you a relative?" she asked, her eyebrow raised.

"No, but I'm the one who stopped the attack. I wanted to make sure she was all right."

"I'm sure the doctor will be by soon, but I'm not sure…"

"I'm a minister," he interrupted her, reaching for the ID he still carried in his pocket.

She looked at him down her nose, her eyes assessing him critically, but she did not take his card.

She turned to him again, her eyes wary. "Listen, I'm not sure if you're telling the truth or not, but you did help. I'll let the doctor speak to you as soon as he's done with her."

"Thank you. I'll just sit over there until he comes."

Without waiting for a response, Daniel turned and headed to the waiting area.

He sat, noticing that he was trembling. He didn't like

hospitals. He closed his eyes and slowed his breathing. But memories from his past kept him from becoming calm.

He saw his wife and his daughter. He heard Lorraine's constant laughter, saw her stomach round with their child. He'd always wondered what she'd seen in him. He had been too serious, too fanatical about his faith. The past few years had taught him that much.

Daniel knew that he'd changed; not only because of the anger that he felt at his loss, but because he had discovered so much about the person he'd been. A lot of it he didn't much care for. He'd been self-righteous and single-minded. Oh, he had been kind to his congregation, but his own family had borne the brunt of his fanaticism.

Yes, Daniel still felt angry with God. He still wondered why his wife and child had been taken away from him.

A noise at the nurses' station distracted him and he turned to see a tall woman standing there, her back to him.

When the nurse pointed at him, she turned and the strangest thing happened. For a moment, he could not breathe.

She moved toward him, her hips swaying from side to side. He did all he could do to control his reaction.

When she reached him, she stopped, a cautious smile on her face.

He immediately stood, not liking the fact that she towered over him while he sat. Now that her head reached his shoulder, he relaxed, feeling more in control.

His standing forced her to step back, but not before he caught a whiff of the fragrance she was wearing. She smelled good, like the freshness after a gentle shower. He almost closed his eyes, feeling the urge to inhale deeply.

She stretched out her hand, shaking his when he accepted her greeting. Pure electricity surged through his body and he did all he could not to release her hand immediately. The startled look on her face made him aware that the touch had affected her in the same way.

"I'm Renée Walker," she said. Her voice was surprisingly strong and husky.

"I'm Daniel Buchanan," he replied.

"The nurse told me that you rescued the young lady?"

"I don't know if I would use the word *rescued* but I was driving home from work when I saw her being pulled into the alley. I had to do something."

"That girl can consider herself lucky. You probably saved her from being raped or killed."

"Is she okay?"

"The doctor examined her a while ago, but she's still suffering the effects of the blow she took. We're still not sure how she is."

"I don't want to be rude, but I'm still not sure who you are," Daniel said.

"Sorry, I should have made it clear from the beginning. I'm one of the hospital's social workers. I'm responsible for cases like this," Renée replied. "She's a teenager and we're going to have to call the police."

"I'm a counselor at The Hope Center on the West Side. I was on my way home from work when I saw her being pulled into the alley."

"A bit late to be out on a cold night like this."

Daniel wasn't sure if it was a comment or a question. He didn't particularly like her tone.

"I work late sometimes."

"Well, I think your work here is done for now. I don't want to keep you out even later. It's almost 2:00 a.m."

"True, it's about time I head home. I just wanted to make sure she was all right."

He turned to walk away, replaying their brief conversation. Leaving now was for the best. He didn't need anyone in his life to complicate it, and this woman already seemed very complicated.

"Wait," her voice called out. "I'll call the Center and let you know how she's doing. And thanks again for helping her. Some people would have just gone on their way. You may have saved her life."

He stared at her for a moment.

"I should be going," he replied. "Thanks for offering to call. I'd like to know what happens to her." Daniel turned to walk away again.

"Hey, sorry to bother you, but can you stop by tomorrow sometime?" she asked cautiously. "She asked for you."

"She asked for me?" he asked, calm and distant.

"Yes, she replied," her voice more pleasant. "I'm sorry, Mr. Buchanan. We have to be careful. I didn't mean to be rude at first. Please accept my apology," she said, her hand outstretched.

He gripped her hand firmly. Her initial skepticism had upset him, but the sincerity in her apology calmed him.

"Yeah, we're fine," he said, turning. And without looking back, he walked away.

Renée closed the door behind her, dropping her bag on the coffee table before collapsing onto the sofa, as she did whenever she entered the apartment after working the night shift.

Fatigue washed over her and she knew it would take strength of mind not to fall asleep right there on the sofa. She needed to take a quick shower. Then she planned to sleep for the next twelve hours before she headed back to work.

She planned on plowing through the piles of paperwork on her desk and finalizing the recommendations she had to submit to the hospital's board. Thank God it was her last scheduled night shift for the rest of the month.

At times like these she was glad she'd made the decision to live near to the hospital. She lived only ten minutes away, unlike some of her coworkers who had to take a long drive out of the city to the suburbs.

Renée assumed that someday she'd have to make that move but for now she was content to be right where she was. She had moved to this apartment when she received the offer from the hospital. She had been surprised, knowing that most of the applicants had been more qualified that she was. She had felt that she'd had a good interview, but she didn't know it had been that good.

She shifted on the sofa, her body aching in places that made her wonder if she was aging faster that she should be. As she sat there, her mind drifted to where she did not want it to go.

The man she'd met tonight. What was his name?

Daniel Buchanan.

She liked him. Just liked him. Nothing more.

Who was she fooling? she thought with a sigh. She'd felt hot and bothered from the moment she laid eyes on him. Tall, dark and handsome.

The stranger had certainly shaken her in a way she didn't much like or understand. He'd stirred her in places she didn't feel were still possible.

Still, she was in no hurry to commit to any relationship, nor was marriage a part of her immediate plans, despite her mother's matchmaking. Maybe in the next fifty years or so. Marriage just didn't mean much to her.

And yet her body continued to betray her, still tingling with awareness. Every nerve ending seemed to remember how he looked, his face animated with concern for the young lady.

What had captivated her most had been his eyes. Pale, liquid amber...an unusual color for a black man.

But Renée had also caught a glimpse of something else in those captivating eyes.

He seemed sad.

She wondered what in his life had caused him such sadness.

* * *

Outside, the cool wind whistled, warning of the colder days to come. Autumn was Daniel's favorite time of year. He loved to see the trees' transformation. In a few weeks, the whole of Chicago would be covered with shades of red, orange and brown.

Today, however, dark clouds filled the city's skyline. There would be a storm that day.

He shifted thoughts of the weather from his mind, replacing them with the vivid image of a woman.

Renée Walker.

He liked the sound of her name on his lips. But another woman's image flashed in his mind.

Lorraine.

Guilt washed over him. For the first time in a long time another woman had tenderly entered his thoughts.

He'd remained celibate after that one disastrous encounter soon after he'd arrived in Chicago. He'd left the woman's apartment feeling as if he had defiled himself. Not because he'd made love to a woman, but because he'd picked her up in a bar and left not knowing her full name.

He'd never been like that. He'd always seen sex as something sacred and intensely spiritual, like the moments of passion he had with Lorraine.

Despite the potential for loss, he missed being in love. He missed sex. He ached for the touch of a woman. He'd loved Lorraine with an intensity he didn't think possible. Though their lovemaking had not been the explosive stuff people talked about, there had been a sweetness and gentleness that had made their intimacy satisfying. That's what he missed the most.

The intimacy and oneness of marriage.

He may be angry with God, but he still knew the meaning of true love. And he didn't think he would ever find it again.

His thoughts again drifted to the social worker and he felt an unexpected stirring in his loins. His body felt alive, as if it were awakening after a long coma. Maybe that's what it was. His body had been in this deadened state for too long.

At the window, the coolness of the wind chilled the heat that burned inside his loins. He stripped, letting his shirt and boxers fall to the ground. His penis hardened and he felt a strange pride. Oh, he had the occasional erection, nature's routine, but never like this.

He turned the lights off, stretched out on the bed and imagined Renée next to him.

He closed his eyes, her scent lingered, so strong… like raindrops on roses. He wasn't even sure if he'd see her again, but he knew in the moment just before he fell asleep that he wanted her and that he *would* see her again.

He urged himself asleep, allowing the tension in his body to dissipate slowly.

Yes, he would.

Chapter 2

On Monday, Daniel finally stepped out of his apartment, his purpose clear. He would see Renée Walker before the day was over.

Because of the constant, heavy rain, he had not left home over the weekend. His body had given in to the need to relax and he'd spent most of the time sleeping.

Chicago seemed refreshed from the rain. The sky sparkled and the trees, lush and vibrant with life, danced in the gentle breeze.

Daniel took the familiar road and headed straight to the center. He noticed that Shelley's car was already there. It was unusual for his boss to arrive before he did. As he stepped into the building, he wondered if something was wrong.

As soon as he entered his office, the intercom beeped. He paused, then answered, "Hello, Daniel Buchanan."

"Daniel, it's Shelley. I saw you come in. Hope you got some rest during your days off, after I had to force you out of here." Laughter was in her voice.

"Yes, I did. My body needed the rest. I spent most of the time sleeping."

"I've been telling you for the longest time that you need to take care of yourself. I'm glad you finally took my advice," she commented.

"Yeah, but I'm sure that's not what you called me about."

"You're right. It's not. A Renée Walker called for you several times. She wants you to call her at the hospital." He could hear the curiosity in her voice.

His heart stopped. He hadn't expected her to call.

"Daniel?"

"Sorry, I'm here. Did she leave a number?"

"Yes, she did. Hold on, let me get it for you."

He heard the shuffling of paper and then she was back. She rattled off a number, which he wrote on his desk pad.

"Remember, you have an appointment with Jerome today," she said.

"I didn't forget. I knew he was back from D.C."

"Good, I have that meeting with the mayor this morning, but when I get back, we have to talk. I have a few things I want to run by you."

"I should be here. I just have to run over to the hospital around five, and then I'll be back to meet Jerome."

"Good, we can talk before you leave for the hospital.

But after your meeting with Jerome, it is home for you. No later than seven o'clock," she insisted. "That's my rule for you. I don't want you in here all hours of the night. That's the night shift's responsibility."

"Fine. Seven it is. I'll be packing up at five minutes to the hour from now on."

Daniel placed the mouthpiece in its cradle, but not before he heard her laughter. He liked Shelley Roberts. She was his boss, but they'd become friends and he knew she valued his contributions to the Center.

In fact, she was the only friend he had.

Yes, he spoke to the other workers, but when he had started there a little over two years ago, he had really connected with Shelley. She'd seen into the hell that was his soul and taken him under her care.

At first he'd tried to keep his distance, but she had refused to allow him to. One day she'd bring cheesecake and then the next a book by one of his favorite authors. He didn't know how she remembered, but he was sure that he had revealed more and more of himself with every conversation, until one night, sitting in her cozy living room, watching one of his favorite movies, he'd broken down and told her all about Lorraine and his daughter.

After that night, their relationship had taken a turn. They'd become solid friends. She was one of the reasons he loved his job as administrator/counselor/mentor. Officially, he was the assistant director of the Center, but all that really meant was that he helped Shelley with everything. But he didn't mind. The Hope Center was a place that gave troubled kids a chance to keep on the straight and narrow.

He caught himself whistling and stopped. Today, he felt different…as if the unexpected awaited him. An eagerness he hadn't felt for years made him pick up the handset and dial the number.

She answered on the second ring.

"Renée Walker. How may I help you?"

"This is Daniel Buchanan." He paused for a response. "You left a message for me to call."

"Oh, Mr. Buchanan. I'm glad to finally reach you. Our Jane Doe is awake and asking for you."

"For me?"

"Yes, she specifically asked for the man who saved her. I've added your name to her visitors' list so you won't have any trouble getting in to see her."

"Is she all right?" Daniel asked.

"She's still having some pain as a result of the concussion. We may have to keep her for a few more days for observation, but she should be okay," Renée replied.

"I'll come over after work today. Around five. I have to be back at the Center by seven o'clock."

"I'm not scheduled to be back at work until tonight, but I can drop by the hospital at four if you can be there an hour earlier. Ask for me at the nurses' station. I want to be there when you talk to her. And thanks for offering to help."

"It's no problem. I'll be there at four o'clock. There's no need to worry. I'm accustomed to working with kids."

"That's good to know. She won't tell us anything about herself. Hopefully, she'll respond better to you."

"I'll see what I can do. I have to go now. I'll see you around four."

"Bye," she said, before she put the phone down.

He liked her voice. It was strong and confident, no nonsense, but, he imagined, holding the promise of more.

Man, what was happening to him?

When he had married Lorraine at twenty-two, he had been a virgin. Not that he hadn't been tempted during their courtship, but they'd both wanted to enter marriage knowing that they had saved themselves for each other.

He laughed. That idea sounded so old-fashioned now, but back then he was innocent and didn't know anything much about the world around him, except the church.

He and Lorraine had fumbled through their wedding night, but over the course of their honeymoon, eager to learn, they'd got things more than right. He'd been shocked by his own passion.

One thing he had to confess was that he loved sex.

He had loved to feel the heat of Lorraine's body under him and at times he'd wondered if they did it too often. But he remembered clearly his father telling him that the marriage bed could not be defiled.

Even now, his body was hardening with arousal. He'd long forgotten how it felt to have a woman close to him, inhaling the scent of her body. Renée's face came to mind instantly.

The sexy temptress/social worker was slowing working her way into his system and she didn't even realize it. He'd felt that moment of awareness between them, could feel it even now.

The thought of seeing her that afternoon energized him, and the day passed with unusual speed. At just after four o'clock, he walked along the corridor of the hospital ward he'd visited the night before. When he reached the nurse's station, about to enquire, he heard Renée's voice behind him.

Time stopped.

Renée stood when she saw Daniel walk down the corridor. He moved with purpose; something that she liked about him. But he seemed a bit too serious, a bit too sad. She'd seen it in his eyes and since meeting him, he'd been on her mind.

Okay, that was an understatement. He'd been in every moment of her day…and night.

Daniel turned at her approach, and she caught a glimpse of something else in his eyes. Something raw.

Fire.

She could feel the heat inside of her, working its way up her body until she could hardly breathe.

He smiled warily and she wondered why.

When she reached him, he smiled again. This time, it reached his eyes.

"Thanks for coming," she said.

"I hope I haven't kept you waiting?"

"No, not at all. I just got here," she responded. "You ready to go see her?"

"Yes, I'm ready when you are."

She stepped off, not looking to see if he followed, but eventually feeling his presence next to her.

She wondered for the hundredth time what it was that made her stomach tie up in knots whenever she thought about this man…a man she'd only seen once before.

Maybe this was what love at first sight felt like. But then she reminded herself she had no intention of falling in love.

"Have you found out who she is?" His question drew her from her reflection.

"No, we haven't found out anything about her."

"Is it the concussion?" he asked.

"I don't think so. I just don't think she wants to talk about herself. Maybe you can help?" Renée said. "She sees you as her hero, her rescuer, her *angel*. Maybe that will give her reason to trust you. I can see that she has lots of stuff bottled up inside and maybe she wants to talk, but she just isn't ready yet."

"I'll see what I can do," he said with determination.

When they reached the girl's room, Daniel waited for Renée to enter.

The girl immediately opened her eyes, her wariness evident, but her attention sparked when she saw Daniel. She smiled, the first smile Renée had seen touch her lips.

Renée remained standing, while Daniel walked forward.

"I hope you're feeling better?" he said.

"I'll be all right," she replied. "It's nothing much. I know how to take care of myself."

Renée saw the bravado and knew that the girl was

more talk than action. The slight trembling of her hand on the bed convinced her of that.

"You can," Daniel said. "I can see that."

The girl's eyes flashed. "I can," she said. "I've been taking care of myself for years."

The fire in her eyes lessened and her voice became shy and softer. "Thanks for coming to help me."

"It's no problem," he assured her. "I've never liked bullies."

She looked at Daniel out of devoted eyes.

"You want to tell me your name?" he finally asked.

She stared at him for a long time before she answered. "Jamie."

Relief swept over Renée. She glanced admirably at Daniel.

"What's your last name?" Renée asked.

Jamie turned to Renée and her expression changed.

"I tell you that and then she'll have me going back where I came from," she accused. "I'm not going back there. I'm seventeen already. I can do what I want."

Renée watched as Daniel reached out and placed his hand on Jamie's. Immediately, she calmed.

"There's no need to be rude," he said. "Ms. Walker is only trying to help you."

Jamie turned toward Renée again. She didn't say anything. Her expression flashed with defiance again.

"I'm going to go to sleep," she said, turning to Daniel. "I'm tired and my head still hurts."

Without waiting for a response, Jamie placed her head on the pillow and closed her eyes.

Renée watched as Daniel stood there for a while,

unsure of what to do or say. Jamie's body needed the rest and time to heal. Her steady breathing soon confirmed that she had indeed fallen asleep.

Daniel finally broke the silence. "Sleep will do her good. You want to go get something to eat? I haven't eaten all day."

Renée hesitated. Going with him was not a sensible thing to do, but she *was* hungry.

"Sure, I haven't had much to eat, either. I'll meet you in the lobby downstairs. I just have to collect my things from my office."

She turned and walked away without waiting for a reply, knowing that his eyes were on her.

Thirty minutes later, awaiting their order, Daniel glanced around the restaurant she'd recommended. He liked the cozy, warm atmosphere. Lively country music flowed from an antique jukebox near the entrance. He'd lived in Chicago for almost two years now, and rarely came to this area since his work and apartment were downtown.

Being here with Renée felt strange, but good. In fact, tonight was the first time he'd been out on a date—if he could call it that—in months.

Sitting opposite him, her hair pulled back in a stiff bun, Renée was the picture of professionalism. She'd taken off her white coat and underneath she wore a business suit, which she didn't seem to realize did little to hide her natural sensuality.

Daniel felt a stirring in his blood. He tried to ignore it.

In the past two days his focus had changed. And it scared him. He'd grown so accustomed to his lack of sexual activity that on the few occasions when nature had demanded release, he distracted himself until the feelings went away.

"So how long have you been living in Chicago?" she asked. Daniel watched as she lifted her glass of wine to her lips, his mind again focused.

"Two years," he replied, intent on being polite if nothing else. "Before that I lived in New York for several years. I'm originally from here, though…a small town called Oak Park, just outside of Chicago."

"I know it. I've been there several times. So what brought you to back to Chicago?"

He hesitated. He'd known somehow that the question would eventually come, but he still wasn't prepared for it. When Daniel finally spoke, he did so slowly. "I just needed a change in scenery."

"It must be a real change from New York. You must miss all the excitement and energy. Did you work in a center while you were there, too?"

"No," he replied. He wasn't sure if he wanted to reveal too much about himself, but her expectant look forced him to respond. "I was a minister at a church in Brooklyn."

The look on her face was priceless.

"*You* were a minister?"

"Yes."

Renée blinked before responding. "You don't look like the minister type."

He laughed and asked the inevitable question. "What does the minister type look like?"

"Well, definitely not like you."

He laughed again. "Sorry, I'm just teasing you. I know what you mean. I've been hearing it for years. If you knew me then, you'd be amazed at how much I've changed."

"What happened?"

"My wife and daughter died in an accident," he blurted out.

He looked at her, watching for her change in expression. He didn't see the expected look of pity, instead, her saw her acceptance and sympathy.

"I'm sorry to hear that. It couldn't have been easy." Her voice was gentle, soothing. A hand reached out and touched his, offering him comfort.

"No, it wasn't. I wandered around aimlessly for a whole year before I shook the grief off and decided to get on with life."

"But it still hurts, I'm sure."

Again, he hesitated. "Yes," he finally replied, "it hurts still, but living each day is a lot easier that it was a year ago. Working at the Center has given me a purpose."

"I'm glad. But, I still can't imagine you standing in a church preaching. You're too…"

She blushed.

"What?" Daniel asked. He wanted to know.

"Sexy," she finally said with a giggle, before she blushed again.

"Oh—oh," he spluttered. He wasn't sure what to say

about that one, but hearing her say it made him feel hot and bothered.

Come on, Daniel. You're losing control.

"I'm sorry," she said. "I didn't mean to embarrass you. My friends always say I speak before I think. I'm sure you'll probably agree."

"Yes, you do. But I'm fine with it. I find honesty refreshing. I may have spent most of my life in church, but it's not easy for anyone to be totally honest."

"A cynical way to look at the world," she observed.

"Cynical, but true. You could say I've earned the right to be cynical."

At first she did not respond. "Because of your wife and child?" she finally asked, cautiously.

"Yes, because of them. But we've talked a bit too much about me. Tell me about yourself."

Before Renée could speak the waitress returned, carrying their meals. After she placed the plates on the table, she smiled, told them to enjoy dinner and left, her eyes focused on Daniel.

"Seems that you have an admirer," Renée said, her voice laced with amusement.

At first, Daniel didn't understand what she was talking about.

"Admirer?" he asked. He seemed more focused on his meal.

"Yes, the waitress."

"You're kidding me. Me?" he asked, his disbelief evident.

"Yes, you."

"Sorry, I didn't notice," he said quickly. "I'm just hungry." He smiled.

He waited until she started before he picked up his knife and fork. They ate in silence, the expressions of satisfaction on their faces evidence of the enjoyment of the simple fare of fried fish and French fries.

When Daniel paused to lay his utensils on the table he said, "So before we started gorging ourselves, you were telling me a bit about yourself."

"Well, you already know I work at the hospital," Renée began. "I'm an only child. My dad died when I was a kid, so it's only my mother and I. My mother is the consummate matchmaker and believes that I will die single and alone. I'm only twenty-eight, so I think I still have some time."

"You were born in Chicago?" he asked, glad the attention was off of him.

"Yeah, I'm a native. Never wanted to live anywhere else. There is nothing like Gino's deep-dish pizza or Garrett's popcorn. Two of my only vices."

"And the hospital? You enjoy working there?"

"Yes, I do. I was fortunate. Just out of college, I applied for a position and got it. I like to work with people, to help them."

"We have that in common. I've always wanted to help people. At first I thought the church was my calling. I wanted to be like my father. Now I realize I can help more people out here doing what I do."

"I wouldn't trivialize the work you did in the church. I'm sure you helped people there."

"Yes, I did, but this is different."

Renée looked at him with curiosity, her eyes boring into his soul. "There is something very heroic about you," she finally said. "What you did for Jamie was remarkable."

"There's nothing heroic about me at all. I just happened to be there at the right time."

"You could have been killed. But you didn't think about what could happen to you—you just did what you thought was right."

"Please don't make me out to be noble," he responded. "I'm far from it. My thoughts right now are far from noble," he confessed with a smirk.

"And what, pray tell, are your thoughts?" she asked, her voice low and husky.

"That I'd like to kiss you."

Everything went still. He couldn't believe he'd said it, but he'd said it and the awareness between them intensified.

"Can we pay the bill and leave?" she asked suddenly.

He wasn't sure what she meant. Had he insulted her?

No, he could see the flame in her eyes.

Renée stared at the television, seeing it but not fully paying attention. Daniel Buchanan's image was firmly locked in her mind's eye.

What was she going to do?

She almost felt like a sinner, but he was not a minister anymore and maybe she needed to pull herself under control. She also noticed the wedding ring on his finger, too. There must still be some attachment to his late wife. That only increased her uneasiness.

She switched the television off, waiting until her vision grew accustomed to the darkness of the night.

Renée touched her lips, closing her eyes and wishing Daniel were there.

Daniel had kissed her.

He'd waited until they reached his car in the dimly lit parking lot and taken her in his arms. His lips had sought hers.

Renée shivered, remembering the intensity of his passion, the touch of his lips on her neck, the probing of his tongue as he parted her mouth.

She'd pressed against him, loving the feel of his body next to hers and the hardness of his arousal pressed against her. She'd almost melted with the heat between them. When Daniel had suddenly pulled away, she had ached for more of him. And then he'd drawn her close to him and held her, placing his arms around her while stroking her hair. When he finally stepped away, she had felt his uneasiness at what they had done.

Renée remained at the window into the early hours of the morning. The kiss had left her aching for more. She was confused, but the only thing clear to her was that she wanted Daniel Buchanan.

Across town, Daniel listened to the gentle pitter-patter of rain. No more heavy downpours and high winds. It was as if nature was apologizing for the past few days of unpredictable weather.

He'd had his meeting with Jerome and was satisfied

that the teenager was progressing well. Daniel still remembered when he'd first met the angry, troubled boy. His instinct had been to take the boy and grip him with a manly hug. He could tell the boy had been hitting out at the world. Later, he'd discovered that all Jerome needed was someone to care about him.

But he still had some concerns about the boy's home life. With only an ailing grandmother, Daniel was worried what would happen if the old lady died. He didn't think Jerome would survive foster care, but the possible alternative was taking his responsibility to another level. He already spent one of his off days, when they fell on Saturday or Sundays, with the boy.

He pushed the thought from his mind. He wasn't ready to be a father to any child. There were too many complications involved, too many issues to deal with.

Daniel had been glad for the meeting. It had kept his mind off of Renée, and the kiss.

Surprisingly, he'd eventually fallen asleep that evening, though he'd lain in bed for hours, thinking about Lorraine…and Renée.

He couldn't believe that he'd just met her three days ago. To say that the kiss had affected him was an understatement. Renée's passion had amazed him, stirring already awakened feelings.

Even now, the taste of her lips caused him to harden, his erection pressing against the tight boxers he wore. He was attracted to her. He'd reveled in her softness, not wanting to let her go and disappointed when the kiss had ended. Even now he still ached with desire.

God, she was beautiful, with that head of luxurious

shiny hair that smelled like a rain-kissed rose. He remained uncertain about what to do. His body told him one thing while his mind said something else.

Getting involved with someone may be a step in the right direction. He'd come to an indifferent understanding of the workings of destiny and fate, but he knew that he was still far from the healing he needed.

Renée Walker could be a meaningful diversion. Daniel wanted to live for today. With Lorraine, he'd envisioned a long future of marital bliss and look where it had ended…with him all alone and broken.

No, he had all intentions of enjoying today. And if enjoying life could be had with a relationship with Renée, then he would explore the possibilities. He knew he wanted more. Wanted to kiss her again. Wanted to feel her legs wrapped around him.

Unfortunately, the guilt he felt each time he thought of her threatened to send him crazy. And if he wanted to see Renée again, it was guilt he needed to resolve.

Chapter 3

The next two days, Daniel visited Jamie at the hospital and felt a sense of disappointment when Renée did not appear. She either hadn't come for the day or she'd already left. He wondered if she was trying to avoid him. And then there was Jamie.

Her slow recuperation worried him. At times she seemed to be healing but other times she continued to suffer from bouts of dizziness and headaches that made her cry. He suspected that the hospital would soon want to discharge her or transfer her to a state hospital, but he planned on talking to Renée about the situation. If he had to pay to make sure Jamie got proper care he would. Very few people knew how well off he was. He'd spent little of the considerable sum of money his father had left him. He and each of his brothers were more than comfortable.

On the occasions when Jamie was in good spirits he tried to get her to open up, but she steered the conversation to trivial things. Still, he knew that eventually she'd open up and tell him the truth.

On Friday, he spent most of the day catching up on his paperwork. In the evening, he had to meet with a group of boys from the local high school, the school Jerome attended. He enjoyed working with these boys. Each of them had been suspended at one time or another from school and had been referred to the Center for counseling. That's how he'd met Jerome.

The Center had been built with boys in mind. In fact, the Center was a facility exclusively for boys at risk. Beyond the office area, there were several activity rooms, two workshops for woodwork, art, crafts, electronics and, of course, a gym with a basketball court. It was there he was heading to meet with the boys.

When he entered, Jerome immediately saw him and nodded in his direction. Daniel returned the greeting and Jerome smiled.

He called the boys in his direction and headed to one of the miniature bleachers. He immediately gave them the good news. They'd qualified this year to take part in a local basketball tournament. Shouts of excitement greeted his announcement.

He continued when the noise finally diminished.

"Basketball practice will begin in a few minutes. I just wanted to talk to you before Coach Bryan arrives. I'm proud of each of you. You've worked hard to achieve this. But not only am I proud of this, I just received your mid-term reports from the school." He paused. "None of you have received a grade below B in any of your classes. That's cause for celebration. So I promise we'll have a party for you after the tournament is over." More cheers and shouts.

"It looks like Coach Bryan has just walked into the gym. It's time to get started. Go warm up."

The boys headed over to the court. Jerome stopped and turned around and returned in his direction.

"I spoke to my homeroom teacher today. I got all A's and a B+. I just wanted to say thanks."

"It's no problem, man. I knew you could do it."

"I couldn't do it without you," Jerome said. He paused. "We won't be able to hang this weekend. I have to meet with a group in my class. We have a project we have to work on."

"That's cool. You have to tell me about your trip to D.C."

"I'll call you later."

"Cool." Daniel nodded. "Got to go play some ball."

Damn, I'm so proud of him, Daniel thought. He glanced at his watch. He still had some time before he headed to the hospital. He would watch some of the practice before he left. His presence also seemed to give the boys a boost. He knew they looked up to him. That was why he often worked long hours. He'd seen too many boys with potential pulled into a life of violence and pain. He planned to do anything in his power to make sure this didn't happen to Jerome or any of the other boys here.

When he finally left the Center, it was with a heart that was soaring. He reached the hospital in record time.

In the elevator, the stillness of the hospital seemed overwhelming, but he didn't feel the usual sense of foreboding. He was too happy to allow anything to spoil his high.

On the fourth floor, one floor before the ward, the elevator stopped and opened, and when Renée stared back at him, he was sure his face showed the same flash of alarm hers did.

She entered, a tight smile on her face.

"Daniel," she acknowledged, her voice distant.

"Renée," he replied.

The door shut behind her, and the elevator went up.

"So how has it been now that you're avoiding me?" he asked, directly.

"Avoiding you?" Her response rushed from her as if she'd anticipated his question.

"Yeah, avoiding me."

"I haven't been," she said. "Why would I be avoiding you?"

"Now that's an interesting question. I have my suspicions, but I'll leave them for when we go out this weekend."

"This weekend?" Renée gasped. "We're going out?"

"Are you going to echo everything I say?"

He heard a clearing throat before he realized the

elevator had stopped and someone was waiting to enter.

Renée stepped out, turning to greet a tall, handsome man as she exited. “Good afternoon, Dr. Haynes.”

“Renée, I visited that girl a few hours ago,” he called after her, his eyes focused on Daniel. “I’m a bit concerned about those headaches she’s been having. I’ve scheduled a few tests for this evening.”

“I saw her a while ago. Daniel’s on his way to see her now.”

“Daniel?” The man’s brow lifted. His tone chilled the area.

“Sorry, this is Daniel Buchanan. He’s the man who rescued her. He works at The Hope Center. Daniel, Dr. Roger Haynes.”

Dr. Haynes stared at Daniel, nodded briefly, his eyes conveying an obvious message.

She’s mine.

Daniel found himself amused by the whole situation. He could tell that the man had made little progress with whatever he hoped for with Renée. He could see it in the tensing of the doctor’s body and the distance Renée maintained between the two of them. There was no intimacy there.

When the doctor finally turned to go, barely acknowledging him, he couldn’t help but chuckle.

Renée turned to him.

“What’s so funny?” she asked.

“Oh, I’ll keep that to myself for a while,” he replied, refusing to give in to the desire to tell her what he thought. "But I promise you, I'll tell you over dinner tomorrow night."

"Are you inviting me out to dinner?" she asked.

"I'm sorry. I should have asked like a gentleman, shouldn't I?" he replied. The laughter was still there. Then his voice became serious. "Renée, will you go out to dinner with me?"

This time she smiled. "I'll think about it, Mr. Buchanan. You have a great evening," she said, her voice laced with laughter.

"I will, Ms. Walker. Call me and let me know your decision."

With that she turned away.

What surprised Daniel was the sense of loss he felt. He'd driven her to that. He'd wanted to anger her, to force her away from him. If he were honest, he'd admit the truth to himself, but even that he did not want to say. To venture there would be to admit so many things he didn't want to admit.

That he was attracted to Renée Walker was a definite.

To say that he lusted after her was a definite.

Surprisingly, how he felt didn't seem wrong. It felt right, totally right.

He was looking forward to dinner. He wanted to kiss her again; needed to kiss her again. Maybe then, he'd be able to work her out of his system.

Daniel turned and headed in the direction of Jamie's room. He greeted the nurse at the nurses' station. She smiled, her eyes sparkling with appreciation. He smiled back.

As he strutted down the dimly lit corridor with its stark white walls, he didn't notice that he'd started to whistle.

Yeah, dinner was going to be interesting.

Two hours later, Renée sat in her office, her annoyance with men evident in her stance. She slammed the empty cup on her desk. She had no idea what was happening to her, but Daniel Buchanan irked her beyond reason. Roger, too, had aggravated her even more. She turned to her best friend.

"So what are you going to do?" Cheryl asked.

"Do about what?" she responded.

"About him?"

"Him?

"The man who has your panties in a bunch," Cheryl said.

"There's no such man."

"Not from what I've heard. Your *boyfriend* called me earlier to find out who "that man" was. So there has to be some man to cause Roger to get all flustered."

Renée fumed inside. What right did Roger have to call Cheryl? She'd made it clear to him on more than one occasion that she wasn't interested.

"Renée? You have that look in your eyes," Cheryl observed.

"What look?" Renée asked.

"That 'I think I hate men' look."

"I do? I assure you it's not that." She stopped. "But the two of them just really pissed me off."

"Even the kindly counselor? I thought you liked him."

"Yes, I do. I like him. He *is* kind of nice."

"Nice? How about sexy and heart-pounding. You look at a man like that and all you see is nice? You must be crazy. Remember, I saw him when he went to visit Jamie. If you don't want him I can take him, but I'm sure he won't be interested in me. And, of course, Julian would have something to say about that."

Renée remained silent for a while.

"I do like him. And he is sexy in a serious kind of way. I haven't felt like this about a man in years and then he just turns up and disrupts my life. I'm not sure if I want to be involved with anyone right now."

"Maybe that's exactly what you need. You've been alone for too long," Cheryl stated. "It's not natural. You can't continue to allow what happened to you so long ago to deprive you of a healthy relationship. And you're too focused on your career. Working yourself 24/7 is not going to warm your bed at night."

"You can afford to say that. You have never been jilted before. And I know you've never had to deal with the men I've had to deal with," Renée added. "You and Julian have been together for almost four years now. I'm sure you'll soon be talking about marriage."

"That proves my point. You can find this, too. Being in love is the most awesome thing."

"I'll take your word for it."

"Come on, you're making me depressed with your attitude. You have a sexy man interested in you and you're playing coy."

Cheryl's cell phone rang. Of course it was one of those sappy love songs. Couldn't people just use the traditional ring?

The grin on Cheryl's face made it obvious that the caller was her dearly beloved. They spoke briefly while Renée concentrated on the work on her desk.

When she flipped the phone shut she turned to Renée.

"I'm so sorry but I have to go pick up Julian at work. His car won't start and he doesn't want to pay a taxi to drive all the way to my apartment when I can pick him up on the way home."

"It's fine. Go."

"You're going to be all right?" Cheryl asked.

"I'm going to be fine. There's a good movie on tonight. And I promised one of the nurses at the hospital that I'd make her a cheesecake for her birthday."

"You and your baking. You should own a restaurant instead of working at the hospital. A waste of talent. You're going to have to invite Mr. Buchanan over the dinner, feed him and spend the rest of the night jumping his bones."

"Don't you have to go pick up Julian?" Renée said, laughing. Cheryl really was outrageous.

"Okay, okay, run me out of your office. We'll pick up this conversation another time."

With that, she stood, waiting for Renée to stand along with her before she hugged her and kissed her on the cheek.

"You take care of yourself. And go out to dinner with the man. He may be your Mr. Right."

* * *

That night, Renée sat on the couch in front of the television. Though one of her favorite shows was on she couldn't focus. Cheryl's words kept popping into her head.

Maybe what her friend was saying was true.

She was tired of being alone, but she also didn't want to take the risk of being hurt. Everyone saw her as being so strong. But she'd had enough bad experiences with love to last her a lifetime and she wasn't sure if she wanted to go back there.

But she was lonely. Renée missed the heat of a man's body next to hers. She missed the fun of doing otherwise ordinary stuff together. But most of all, she missed that special communication that comes with being in love.

Oh, yes, she had been in love before.

But the day she'd sat outside the church in a limousine waiting for her soon-to-be-husband to arrive, realizing that he wasn't coming, she'd vowed never to fall in love again.

Sure, she'd had relationships over the years. A consenting adult, she'd enjoyed sex, but that was it. She'd never experienced the heart-pounding, toe-curling lovemaking that Cheryl kept telling her about, and a part of her wanted it.

Her phone rang and she picked it up, too lazy to look at the display to see who was calling.

"Hello."

"Renée, Daniel here."

Her heart missed a beat.

"Yes, Daniel," she replied. "How can I help you?"

"Jamie would like to talk to you. She said she didn't see you today."

"Is something wrong?"

"No, but she says that you're the only woman she will talk to."

"Okay, I'll go see her first thing in the morning."

"Good, which leads me to the second reason I called. Are you still willing to have dinner with me?"

She hesitated at first, but then replied. "You did eventually ask, didn't you." She paused before she spoke again. "Yes, I'll have dinner with you."

"Good, thanks for accepting. Now, why didn't it go like that the first time around?" he asked.

"Maybe because the first time you didn't ask me like a gentleman should," she replied. "But I'll overlook that minor infraction. I'm looking forward to dinner."

"I'll pick you up at seven tomorrow night, if that's fine with you?"

"Yes, that's fine."

"I'll see you later. And Renée?"

"Yes."

"I have all intentions of kissing you again."

With that Daniel put the phone down. Renée experienced the familiar tingle of anticipation and excitement.

Dinner was going to be interesting.

Daniel rested the handset on the cradle and chuckled. *That* would leave her all flustered and bothered for a while.

Renée had been on his mind all day and his need to

be with her was intensifying. He liked the feeling, but he was worried about how quickly it was developing. Just a few days ago, he'd been dealing with the past and here he was obsessed with a woman he had just met. He couldn't help himself. Her image haunted him and his body burned for her. Maybe, he'd been without a woman for too long. The kiss they'd shared had aroused emotions that he wasn't sure he wanted to handle. Their coming together was unavoidable.

And if he had anything to do with it, it'd be sooner than later.

Chapter 4

During the night, images of Daniel Buchanan filled Renée's dreams. Several times she awoke, her body alive with the memory of his kiss.

She tried to purge his image, but nothing she did worked. Once, she tried counting sheep, but soon they morphed into him, a situation that only served to increase her irritation with him, a man she hardly knew….

In the stillness of the room, Renée laughed, knowing that her attraction to him hinted at her need for companionship. Yes, she spent most of her time running away from relationships, but none of her mother's finds or the men of her acquaintance stirred her like Daniel Buchanan did.

Even though he'd told her, and she knew he was being

honest, she couldn't understand what it would be like to lose someone you loved the way he did. Her memories of her father had faded and even when he'd passed away, she'd been too young to feel anything much.

His wife and daughter.

He'd said it so matter-of-factly, but she'd seen the flash of hurt. She reached out and touched him, hoping she'd given him comfort. His only response had been to squeeze her hand.

Life was so complicated and frustrating. She'd stayed away from men for so long and now she found herself drawn to a man who needed her to comfort him and help him to heal. Well, that was what she was going to do. She'd help him. She wanted to see him really smile. He needed to live again.

She had looked at him just like she looked at all those cases she'd had to deal with. Just another case, another person to counsel and help. She was going to help him and starting tomorrow would be perfect. She'd keep her eyes off his bulging muscles, and the uncertain smile that flickered briefly in the amber pools of his eyes. She'd never seen a man with eyes that color, but his almost made her drunk with their power.

An image of her lying under him flashed in her mind's eye, vivid and bold, and she closed her eyes, the sweetness of arousal washing her body with its heat. Renée reached for the reading lamp on the side table and flicked the switch on. Maybe, a good book would help.

An hour later, despite her attempt to immerse herself

in the latest mystery from her favorite author, the image of Daniel Buchanan still haunted her.

On Saturday, when Daniel saw Renée, he couldn't help but be taken aback by her beauty. But he suspected she didn't care too much about that part of her. Not that she didn't dress and carry herself well, but she seemed oblivious to her own ability to turn a man's head.

Since seeing her, he'd spent Thursday and Friday thinking about her, especially after she'd called to tell him she had an emergency and could not accept his invitation to dinner. He'd even experienced a sense of relief when she'd not been at the hospital when he visited Jamie yesterday.

Now, he could not help but stare at her as she stood talking to one of the doctors. He could tell she was angry, but struggled to control her composure. He could see determination etched on her face. He watched her, enjoying the way she became so animated when she talked. She used her hands and body to emphasize her point. And then she turned in his direction and something strange and unexpected happened.

He felt alive.

Fire blazed inside. Not just the flame of desire, but something more, something exciting. He immediately sought to control his body.

She turned to the doctor, said something to him and then headed in his direction. From the redness on the doctor's face, Daniel suspected she'd scored the winning goal.

When she reached him she smiled, but he could tell

that she was angry about what had happened between her and the doctor.

"Daniel," she acknowledged.

"Renée," he responded, amazed that he sounded so calm when inside his heart raced so quickly.

"Jamie has been moved from the room I assigned her. She has no insurance. I tried to see if I could get something worked out but that…idiot has already moved her."

"But she's still in the hospital, right?"

"Yes, she is."

"Then there is no need to be feeling like you do. He didn't put her out."

"Sorry, I try not to get emotional about patients, but it's easier said than done. Especially if it's a young girl."

"Remember, I work with kids, too, and there is no day when I don't feel like I'm fighting against the rigid bureaucracy. So I do know exactly how you feel."

"You're right. I need to cool down a bit, I suppose," she replied.

"You're going up to see her now?" he asked.

"No, I just came from seeing her. I'm on my way downtown to a meeting."

"So what about dinner?" he asked. "I was disappointed you couldn't make it the other night."

Renée looked at him strangely and replied, "I really did have an emergency."

"I understand, but we *do* need to talk about Jamie. I'd like to find out who she is, who her parents are."

"Okay, we can still do dinner, but it is going to be strictly business," she said firmly.

He couldn't help but smile. "I promise," he said, knowing she must have heard the laughter in his voice.

She looked at him strangely, and then tried to plaster a stern expression on her face.

"I'm not sure I like the look on your face. I'm tempted to conduct business with you only in my office, but I haven't eaten out in a week, so it'll be a nice change. So don't think it's because I want to spend any time with you."

"I won't think that at all. Now I can get back to work and you can get on to your meeting. I suggest you be getting on your way."

She smiled, turned quickly and walked away, the sway of her hips drawing him like a magnet.

Yes, he could see that he was in trouble. She was nothing like his wife. Lorraine had been a beautiful woman, but he could never define her as sexy. Yes, they'd made love often and sometimes passionately, but sometimes he'd felt like she was being the dutiful Christian wife, and he had been happy with that.

Now Renée tempted him in a totally unexpected way. She didn't even seem aware of the effect she was having on him.

He finally moved, heading toward the elevator. A short ride later, he was stepping out and moving toward the nurses' station. He'd forgotten to ask Renée for Jamie's new room number.

"Hi," he told the older nurse. "I'm trying to find the

room number for a patient. Her name is Jamie Fenty. I'm not sure of her previous room number, but she was brought into the hospital last week. Renée Walker will vouch for me if you call her."

"That's no problem, Mr. Buchanan. We all know who you are. You may have saved that girl's life. She's in room 402."

"Thanks," he replied. So they were calling him some kind of hero. He really didn't like that.

Back down the elevator and four floors below, he entered the ward. The room held three beds. One was empty, the other held a sleeping woman. Jamie, oblivious to the world, seemed engrossed in the book she was reading. Despite that, she must have heard his footsteps. She turned in his direction and then quickly looked away, but not before he saw the flash of happiness.

"Nice to see you, too," he said.

Her head turned, and she stared at him for a long time before she spoke.

"Isn't your time for being a hero over?" she said, her voice laced with sarcasm.

For some reason he wanted to reach out and hug her and tell her everything was going to be all right, but he suppressed the feeling. He didn't want to feel like this, didn't want to care. So why was he here? Why did he keep coming back?

"So is there something wrong with caring about people?"

She started to speak, but stopped abruptly. She hadn't expected his response.

"Care? You're just being sly. You're just like all those

other guys. Rescue me, be nice and then take what you want? You want a freebie?"

She continued to look at him and her stare didn't waver. Neither did his. He couldn't let her think he was weak. Eventually, she looked away.

"I'm tired. My head hurts," she said, her face showing her discomfort. "I need to get some sleep. You can go. Your good deed for the day is done. God must be pleased with you."

"I'm sure he's pleased with you, too. You seem to have been a bundle of joy for the day. I've been told you've been surly to the nurses."

And then she laughed, a loud heartfelt laugh that transformed her from a scared little girl hidden behind a wall of bravado, into an angel.

It was unexpected and he just watched her, until she stopped, her wall rebuilt higher.

"Don't say anything."

"I wasn't going to," he said.

"You always seem to want the last word."

"Seems that I *am* getting the last word. Comes with years of practice."

She did not respond, only rested her head back onto the pillow. Daniel could see that she was avoiding responding.

"Look, I just came to check in on you. I need to get home now."

"Have a big date?" she said with a sly smile.

"In fact, I do."

"With Ms. Walker?"

He felt the heat against his face, but responded.

"Now that is certainly not any of your business. You have a good night," he said and turned to leave, but not before he saw the laughter in her eyes, the same loud uninhibited laughter, and it made him happy. Before he closed the door, he looked back. Her eyes were still on him. "I'll be back tomorrow and the next day, and the day after that. Be sensible and get accustomed to it. You won't drive me away."

The look of bewilderment on her face was priceless.

He turned and walked away. At least he knew she'd got his message.

Renée put the phone down. She finally called him to let him know she could go out with him on Sunday, after having had to cancel their date on Friday night.

She wanted to go, but an emergency at work had forced her to remain there well into the evening. She wanted to get to know him. It wasn't about her attraction to him. That was a given, but she knew the best way to deal with what was happening.

She'd use their time together to find out about him. What made him seem so controlled and caused those occasional glimpses of sadness.

She shook her head, rose from the stool and walked over to the oven. The decadent whiff of chocolate chip cookies filled the room. Before the night was over, they'd all be gone.

Renée poured a glass of milk, a nightly habit, and walked to the sitting room. For some reason cookies and milk seemed to be the only thing to calm her, and tonight, her trepidation at the upcoming date left her feeling edgy.

She used a remote control to turn the home theater system on. Strains of smooth jazz filled the room. Perfect for her milk and cookies and the perfect time to look over the important cases she had to deal with; allowing her mind to focus on something besides Daniel Buchanan.

Sometimes she wondered why she continued to do the work she did. Working with children and teenagers haunted her at night.

Where had her childhood dream of being a singer gone?

She'd woken up some time in high school and realized that life was more than a great voice. That she wanted to help people. She'd known that being a doctor had been out of the question. She and blood did not mix and it had taken her a while to accept that she could not do what her mother wanted. In fact, she'd finally realized that much of what she had wanted to do had been what her mother wanted her to do. She realized now that she'd found a purpose for living.

And that was what she planned to do with Daniel Buchanan. Help him on the road to recovery. She could tell that he'd suffered, but with time she knew that she could help him to heal.

Without warning the phone rang, making her jump with its shrill ring.

She had already picked it up when she checked the caller ID and saw that it was Cheryl.

"Yes, girlfriend. I did promise I would call. What you doing?" Cheryl asked.

"Eating. Reading."

"Cookies, right?" Cheryl asked, her voice expectant.

"I confess."

"Chocolate chip?"

"Yes."

"Girl, want some company?'

"Sure. But if you want some of these, I suggest you get over here soon."

"I'll be right over. And please make sure you keep a plate full for me."

Forty-five minutes later, Cheryl opened the door with her spare key and entered, her hands laden with several bags and a large box.

"Chinese," she responded when Renée raised her brow. "I know for sure that if I didn't bring something else for you to eat, you'd settle for those cookies for dinner. Cookies are dessert, Renée. How many times do I have to tell you that eating all those sweets will be your downfall?"

Renée laughed. "Look who's talking?" she accused. "It's a good thing I've encouraged you to join the gym. At least we get to work off all those calories."

"Well, let's not waste time chatting. Where are those suckers?"

They both laughed.

"Come, let's get a couple sodas, watch a movie and have dinner. Of course, those cookies are dessert."

"I'm with you, girlfriend. Something exciting and fun. No soppy romance for me."

Several hours later, tired but not ready to sleep, Cheryl finally got down to business.

"So how's the ex-minister?" Cheryl asked.

"Now, why do you have to go there?"

"You know me. I can't resist a sexy man, even if he was a minister. And note, the word is *was*. So you plan on jumping his bones."

"Cheryl!" Renée said with a laugh.

"Don't Cheryl me. I'd have had his body all racked and exhausted ten minutes after meeting him. You'd think he was created so beautiful for nothing. I mean, he's a bit too serious for my liking, but he's one hot specimen of manhood."

"You are so dirty, girl. Is sex the only thing you think about?"

"Of course not. Not when I can take home a few of those cookies you have left over."

They laughed. Then Cheryl got serious and looked at her with a stare that suggested she knew exactly what was going on in Renée's head.

"So you like him?"

There was no sense in denying what was obvious to her friend.

"Yes, I like him," she replied. "Cheryl, you know me. Relationships and I don't work."

"I know it hasn't been easy, but suppose you were to find happiness with him? He seems like a good guy."

"I don't believe he's ready for any kind of relationship yet. He's a widower. His wife died just three years ago."

"But I see the way he looks at you."

"Look, I like him, but nothing is going to happen between us. And I'm definitely not interested in a relationship. Besides, he needs help. He needs someone to help him deal with his wife's death. I suspect that he hasn't yet. I'm sure he still loves her."

"You know what you need? A good curl your toes session of uninhibited sex."

Renée rolled her eyes.

"Don't roll your eyes at me. Lately, everything for you is work."

"And you don't spend all your time at the hospital?"

"Yeah, I do, but at least I'm getting some when I'm not there."

"Maybe you're right," Renée said. "Maybe I do need to concentrate on my life outside of work a little more."

"Now, that's my girl," Cheryl said happily.

For a while there was silence, and then they looked at each other and smiled.

Chapter 5

Renée took her time dressing. She'd found the perfect little number in her closet—a dress she had purchased on a whim a few months ago. Despite the cost, she couldn't resist the earthy tone of the Ellen Tracy design.

Now, looking at herself in the mirror, she realized she had made the right choice. The dress fit her perfectly, accentuating her slenderness. Its color complemented her mahogany hair, which she'd left loose, instead of secured in the serviceable bun she usually wore to work. Renée knew she looked her best. She'd often wished she had the height and body of a model, but the face looking back at her was attractive.

She turned away from the mirror, glancing at the clock on the bureau—another twenty minutes before Daniel arrived. Renée felt her hands tremble. She looked back at the mirror. She hoped Daniel didn't get the wrong impression. She looked ready for seduction, but that was not the first thing on her mind. She just wanted to look good.

The sound of the doorbell echoed in the distance and she grabbed her bag and coat and hurried to the door. There, she paused, breathing deeply, finding control. She opened it…and almost lost it.

Daniel was beautiful.

He oozed sinful sex and she wondered again how on earth he could have been a minister.

He reached behind his back and handed her a small, short-stemmed, pink rose, soft and pale.

She took it from him, her body tingling when his hand brushed hers.

"Thank you. I love roses," she said. She placed it in her hair.

"Is it okay?" she asked.

"You look lovely."

She smiled and thanked him again.

"You ready to go?" he asked.

"Whenever you are, I'm ready." She wanted to ask where they were going, but decided that she preferred to be surprised.

"Do you like soul food?" he asked, while she locked the front door.

"I love it," she responded.

"Good," he said with delight. "Have you ever been to Edna's?" At her nod, he continued. "I try to eat there as often as I can. There is nothing like Edna's biscuits."

She smiled. "I know what you mean. Or the peach cobbler. I can almost taste it."

"I'm glad you like my choice."

They reached his car and he moved to open the door for her. She pulled her coat closer. It was a typical autumn night, a cool wind blowing through her hair. She shivered. She could do with some heat.

When she slipped inside the car, the warmth of the heater was welcome, but when his leg touched hers, the resulting heat, which coursed through her body, was overwhelming. Renée tried to focus ahead, trying to ignore to feel of his leg on hers.

For a while they drove in silence.

"You seem to enjoy your work," he said firmly.

"Yes, sometimes, but the bureaucracy often makes it difficult. Even this case with Jamie is frustrating me. I have a few days to find accommodations for her. There is some state funding for cases like hers. Fortunately, the headaches she's been having are less frequent. The medication seems to be working."

"I'm going to see her tomorrow," he said. "She's talking to me but she still hasn't said too much about herself. And if the funds are a problem, I can cover the hospital bill."

"Well, that may not be necessary yet, but it's extremely kind of you to offer. You seem to be good at this kind of work. Talking to people."

"Came with past territory. I did spend the first fifteen years of my life after college as a minister. Counseling comes second nature."

"Why did you stop being a minister?" she asked.

When his body stiffened noticeably, she realized she had touched a nerve.

"I didn't have much use for God in my life anymore. I wanted to do something else," he said without emotion.

"I'm sorry, I didn't mean to pry."

"You're not prying. It's just something I don't talk about much. I've learned to deal with it."

"You've been working at the Center for how long?"

"About two years. Before that I did a bit of drifting from city to city."

Renée wanted to ask more questions but suspected that she shouldn't. The tension in the car was like a pall, so she decided against pushing the issue. She didn't want the evening to be over before it even started.

His reaching over to turn on the radio only confirmed her suspicions. His past was definitely off limits.

"What's your pleasure? R & B, jazz, pop?" Daniel asked.

"Jazz, definitely."

"My thoughts exactly."

Soon the sultry voice of Anita Baker filled the car. Maybe something so romantic was not the best choice, but it did take her mind off their brief conversation. Someday she'd really have to press him if she planned on helping him deal with whatever has affected his life so much.

They remained quiet for the rest of the drive, the music helping to soothe their troubled thoughts, but both very aware of each other. Tension crackled in the silence of the car's interior. While he drove, she couldn't keep her eyes from straying in his direction.

When the car pulled into the parking lot of the restaurant, Renée exhaled deeply, trying to hide her relief. If she'd stayed in the car for another minute, she was sure she would have begged him to take her right there in the car. Her attraction to him continued to startle her with its power. Her whole body felt alive. The woodsy scent of his cologne tempted her with its masculine subtlety and she ached to draw near to him, bury her head in his chest and inhale deeply. She closed her eyes. If she wasn't careful, she would probably end up in bed with him. But she was smarter than that. She may be attracted to the sexy ex-minister, but she was strong and determined not to make love to him.

Not tonight.

The atmosphere in the restaurant was perfect. The food was great, the music was seductive, the company was appealing. Daniel couldn't keep his eyes off Renée.

He wasn't sure what was going on. Maybe it was the two glasses of wine, maybe it was the fact that all night long he'd inhaled her sweet scent until his blood boiled with a passion he had not felt in a long time. He knew he was attracted to her, but he'd been able to control his feelings in her presence…until tonight.

Across from him, she lifted the spoon to her lips, sipping the spicy West Indian soup. He enjoyed watching her eat. She didn't play around with her food but savored every morsel that passed her lips.

"You going to have dessert?" he asked, handing her the menu.

Renée browsed it for a while and then handed it back to him.

"Peach cobbler, right?" he asked again. "I can see you have a sweet tooth," he said. "One only has to see the look of utter satisfaction on your face. It's a..."

"It's a what?" she asked, an eyebrow lifted.

"I think maybe it's best if I don't say."

"Chicken," she teased.

"I was going to say, it's a real turn-on."

She looked at him, and he could tell he'd shocked her.

"I didn't expect that to come from you."

"Why? Because I was a pastor?"

She hesitated. "Yes, forgive me, but I find it so hard to visualize you standing in front of a congregation preaching the good news."

"If you'd known me a few years back, you definitely wouldn't have liked me that much. I wasn't the nicest of people. Definitely a little too self-righteous. I believed that I could do nothing wrong, but condemned everyone, even my own family. But I loved the work I did. I'm a lot more *human* these days." He leaned forward. "But let's change the subject. I've been watching you eat all night and wishing your mouth were on me."

He watched her gasp. But he wanted to be honest.

"Right now, I want to take you back to my apartment and make love to you all night."

She finally spoke. "You are very direct, I must say."

"Maybe I am. But life is too short to waste time beating around the bush. Not that I do this often. In fact, I don't do this at all. But I'm attracted to you and I want to make love to you. I promise you it won't be a one-night stand. I don't do one-night stands."

"That's good to know. I guess I'm going to be getting dessert after all," Renée said with a wink.

Dessert indeed.

"I'll get the hostess so we can get out of here," Daniel said.

Outside, the wind blew gently. The moon, at its fullest, glowed in the night sky.

Daniel unlocked the car and opened the door for her. Before she stepped inside, he pulled her against him. He needed to kiss her and couldn't wait until they arrived at her apartment. Heat raced through him as he kissed her hard and deep, not wanting to stop. Her heart beat rapidly against his chest. Reluctantly he pulled away, breathing as deeply as she did.

"Come on, let's go," he said, his voice husky with his desire.

Renée nodded, unable to speak. Desire flamed in her eyes.

The drive back to her apartment took longer than he wanted, and the thought of what was about to happen kept him on edge. He didn't say much, instead focusing on the road ahead. There was no need for idle chitchat. Instead Anita Baker continued to set the mood for the unfolding seduction.

Daniel felt alive with anticipation. He could already

feel himself deep inside her, and he did all he could to stop himself from groaning with desire.

Daniel practically kicked her door in, his mouth still covering hers. He didn't want this to stop. He knew he might regret it in the morning, but tonight he wanted her and that was all that mattered.

The light came on, illuminating the room.

"Where's the bedroom?" he asked, feeling empty when he took his lips from hers.

"The door to the left," she replied.

She uncoiled from around him, held his hand and he followed. In the bedroom they stood in the darkness.

"Turn the light on."

She did and then turned to him. She stood bold, the initial uncertainty gone. He moved to the center of the room and she followed him. He stopped, looked down at the bed and noticed its pink frilliness.

She came up behind him, her body barely touching his, but he could feel her heat.

He turned to face her.

He wondered for the hundredth time if he was doing the right thing, but then he felt her hand on him, cupping his erection through his pants, and all his reservations faded.

"Yes, touch me. I want your hands on me," he groaned.

Her hands tugged at his zipper, slowly easing it down. His pants fell to the floor, revealing the loose boxers he wore, but they did little to hide his arousal. Those, too, slipped to the floor.

She cupped his length in her hands again, and then gently stroked him.

He reached down, stilling her movement. "Hold on," he said. "First let's get you out of this."

He removed her dress with a quickness he didn't realize he had, and she soon stood naked before him. She was beautiful, more than beautiful. Renée had lovely breasts. Not too big, not too small. Just right.

He reached out and touched them, loving the way her body trembled and her nipples perked.

She wanted him. He could tell and there was an unexpected pride in that knowledge. A flash of guilt stuck in his throat, but the sight before him was too much to ignore and the feeling lessened to a nagging somewhere in the background of his consciousness.

Daniel sat on the bed, moving her to stand between his legs, her breasts at eye level. He cupped one breast and one stiff nub into his mouth, his teeth tugging, pulling and giving rise to sweet groans of pleasure.

His other hand too found the gentle mound at the parting of her legs, and he slipped his hand inside, his fingers working magic as she trembled from head to toe.

He heard her whisper, "I want you," and knew he could not contain himself anymore.

He placed his mouth on hers again, slipping his tongue inside, wanting the intimacy that came from contact with a woman. But he didn't want any woman.

He wanted Renée.

He hoped this encounter would quench his thirst for her, but immediately he knew he wouldn't be satisfied with a one-off solution to the problem. He wanted more, needed more.

For the briefest of moments, his late wife's face flashed in his mind, but he dismissed her. He didn't want this to be about her. He wanted to do this without any guilt, without a sense of dread.

He groaned. Her mouth had found its way to one of his nipples.

His body responded immediately as he felt a bolt of heat rush through him as his penis hardened further still, until the pain of his erection was almost unbearable.

He pulled away, lowering her to the bed, then he poised himself above her.

She reached into her nightstand for a condom and placed it in his hand.

"Put it on for me," he commanded.

She complied. Her hands were gentle on him. He'd loved the sensation that soared through his body. There was an intimacy about a woman rolling the cool latex on him that turned him on. The feel of her hand on his length evoked a groan, but he breathed in deeply, gaining control again.

When she was done, he positioned himself between her legs, slowly guiding himself inside her. Her slick wetness drew him in, allowing him to slip smoothly inside. She felt perfect.

He remained still for a while, trying to gain control. He wanted to savor the moment, the incredible feel of her body. She wiggled beneath him, trying to get accustomed to his size and hardness.

"Please," she said.

Daniel didn't need any more encouragement. He moved slowly inside her, stroking her long and deep. Her legs widened, allowing him more access to her, a deeper penetration, until he felt they were completely joined and her body had become a part of his.

Her body moved under his, a slow, circular movement completely in sync with his actions, almost as if their bodies already knew each other intimately.

When her legs moved and wrapped around his waist, he lost all control and he increased his pace. He needed release. He shortened his strokes, moving quicker and harder inside her, her moans urging him on. And then it happened, as he expected, the sudden clenching of his abs, the tingling along his spine and the tensing of his legs. He felt his release even before it started. His manhood expanded and then spasm after spasm of pure pleasure ripped through his body.

He heard a howl and realized it was his voice. She followed him with her own cry of ecstasy; her legs gripped him tighter as she joined him. Finally, control restored, he held her tight as she shuddered and convulsed against him, her eyes opened wide with the wonder of what she was feeling.

When she finally relaxed, he continued to hold her, afraid to let her go, afraid that this was all a dream, afraid he'd wake up to the cold hard reality of his life.

Chapter 6

During the night, Renée woke to a sense of stillness and loneliness. Outside, the sounds of Chicago at night comforted with their familiarity. She turned to the man who lay next to her.

What had she done?

She wasn't sure how she felt, but she did know she'd experienced the best sex she'd ever had in her life.

Renée slipped out of the bed. She needed to get away from him. Fear like nothing she'd ever experienced before held her tight in its grip and she stumbled out of the bedroom, turning the light in the living room on to erase the darkness.

She moved toward the balcony, sliding the door open when she reached it. She stepped outside, inhaling the cool night air. Her heart was still racing and she slowly brought it under control. She was afraid.

She couldn't explain her feelings for him. Every time she thought of him, she felt even more confused. He was definitely not her usual kind of man. She'd always been attached to the more outdoorsy type or the witty extrovert. Daniel was the strong silent type.

But acknowledging that didn't negate how attractive and sexy she found him. His calm, controlled demeanor masked a man holding his passion in. She knew it… knew that there was something profoundly deep and emotional within him. She'd caught a glimpse of that man tonight. She'd caught a glimpse of the heat he tried to keep dormant inside.

Not that she was complaining. Their lovemaking had been wonderful, yet she could tell he'd been holding back, and she found herself wanting all of him.

In the distance, the night lights of Chicago flickered. She loved the city—its vibrancy and its atmosphere. Though she'd considered jobs elsewhere, she could never leave. When Vincent Memorial had offered her the job, she had jumped at the chance, even though the pay would have been lower than some of her other offers. Being happy wasn't always about money.

She closed her eyes, soaking in the feeling of the Chicago midnight. She needed to get back to bed. She had to work the early shift in the morning, and she hated to be late.

Renée returned to the bedroom. Daniel was still sleeping. She laughed. She'd tired him out. She felt the same; he had been a demanding lover.

She slipped between the sheets, drawing closer to him. She loved the feel of his body next to hers…the hardness, the strength, the way her heart rate quickened with excitement and anticipation. She was madly attracted to him and that alone scared her.

And then she realized he had stopped breathing, and two eyes flaming with fire stared at her. Instinctively, she reached up and kissed him on the nose, and gasped when he responded by capturing her lips.

Under the covers, she felt his arousal against her stomach and she reached out, holding him in her hands. His penis jerked and she felt pride in knowing that he responded to her. He was large and she was amazed that she'd accommodated him so well. She loved the fullness of him inside her and her body ached to feel him again. She ran her hands along his thick length, loving the feel of its ridged texture. He moaned, a vulnerable sound that made her know she was in control.

She felt the gentlest of touches at her womanhood. Her hand covered his, and she widened her legs, giving him the access he wanted, that she wanted, too.

A finger slipped inside her tenderly, finding her sensitive nub. His finger teased it and she released him, her palms folding and opening with the sensation that washed over her. She bit her lips trying to keep the sound in but with every flick of his finger she knew the sweetness of pain.

Daniel removed his hand and she almost screamed in protest, but when his head moved between her legs, she stopped, knowing what was to come would be even better. He placed his mouth on her, his tongue slipped between the delicate folds, and he made love to her in a way she'd never experienced before. All she could do was give in to the thrill surging through her body and enjoy the skillful way he pleasured her.

And then he stopped and raised himself above her and prepared to enter her for the second time that night. Again she almost screamed with the impact of his entry. But her body was ready and when he pulled back and stroked her again, she met him halfway, joining him with a fervor of her own. She groaned and cried at each firm, hard stroke, wrapping her legs around him, and drawing him closer.

She clenched her muscles around his penis, wanting to give him as much pleasure as she could.

While they made love he whispered to her. Words of pleasure, naughty words that teased her, urging her to do what he wanted. And she responded willingly, titillating him in her own way.

Then she felt it…that awesome sensation that started deep inside and worked its way to the surface. Her body begged for release and then he screamed her name as his body shuddered with the chill of his orgasm.

Seconds later she joined him, unhappy that it was over, but allowing the waves of pleasure to take her floating on a cloud before she found herself falling once again into sleep.

When Daniel awoke he was disoriented for a moment, but the woman next to him brought back images of the night before. He glanced toward the window. The sun, barely awake, cast its pale rays of soft shades of orange and yellow across the morning sky. A glance at the dull neon glow of the clock on the wall confirmed that it was just after seven o'clock.

Renée sighed in her sleep and drew closer to him. His arousal was immediate.

He wanted to make love to her again, and knew if he woke her, she'd melt in his arms. He liked lying next to her, but he needed to go to the bathroom. He slipped out of the bed, trying to make sure that he didn't wake her. He wasn't sure where the bathroom was, but he suspected it was the door on the left. He was right, and it took a bit of fumbling to find the light switch. And then he saw it…glistening on his finger.

His wedding ring.

The ring he'd worn for the last ten years. The ring his late wife had placed on his left hand. He felt a guilt so strong and so heavy, he could sense the telltale prick of tears.

He reached to take it off, but found he couldn't. Taking it off would be to break the final link to Lorraine. He knew immediately he'd made a mistake and promised himself that he'd never do this again.

And yet, while his love for Lorraine still existed, his feelings for Renée went deeper than he expected, than he wanted. It was too soon. He felt as if he had cheated on his late wife and she was looking down at him from above.

To love again was a definite no-no, and this "thing" with Renée was definitely heading that way. He didn't want this. He'd already lost his wife and his daughter. He couldn't lose anyone again. He couldn't deal with the pain. Lorraine's and his daughter Chelsea's deaths had devastated him and he couldn't tell what the loss of someone else would do to him.

He had to leave.

He went back into the bedroom. She was still asleep. He searched for his clothes on the floor, disentangled them from hers and slipped them on. He stood staring down at her for a long time, then he turned and exited the apartment. Instead of going directly home, he drove until the sun peeped over the horizon, until it was high above him.

Had he done the right thing? He wasn't sure, but for now he knew that he couldn't be with her. Despite the progress he had made in the past few years, he was not a whole man yet. He would be the first to admit that.

Until he'd dealt with his hurt and his pain, he couldn't love again and Renée deserved better. She deserved someone who could truly love her. He couldn't give her that yet, when memories of his wife still lingered.

When Renée opened her eyes, she immediately noticed that Daniel was gone. Somehow she'd expected it. Her life seemed to unfold like the scenes from one of those melodramatic soap operas that so many women loved to watch during the quiet afternoon hours.

She rose from the bed, her body still alive with the lingering touch from his hands. She looked around for her clothes. They were neatly folded on the sole chair in the room.

She headed to the bathroom, needing to take a shower. Her body ached, weary from the passionate exertion. But she felt good, alive. If Daniel had wakened her and made love to her again, she would have welcomed him into her body without hesitation.

And therein lay the problem. Or, therein *didn't* lay the problem, more appropriately.

She was falling in love with Daniel Buchanan. She didn't want to. She knew that she shouldn't. She'd only met him a week ago. Things were moving much too quickly.

He was still in love with his wife. That much she knew. She'd noticed again the ring on his finger, evidence of his devotion to a woman who'd died.

And she could do without relationships. Love was the stuff in romance novels that ended happily ever after. In real life, love could be there, but so many factors existed that challenged its chance of survival.

She turned the shower on full blast, allowing the water to feel like needle pricks on her body. She welcomed the harshness, and it soothed her. It was something she needed. And then it happened, the unexpected.

She started to cry. Fast-flowing, uncontrollable tears that she wasn't even sure had a reason to appear. Maybe she could no longer deny the loneliness that defined her existence. Maybe Daniel's entrance into her life had only made her aware of all that was missing. Maybe it was those feelings she thought she had buried since her abrupt return to singlehood several years ago.

For so long she had not wanted a man, but Daniel Buchanan had changed that. He affected her in ways she could not understand.

Turning the water off, she stepped out of the shower

and headed back to the bedroom. She dried her skin quickly and changed the sheets on the bed. Daniel's scent lingered everywhere.

Sighing in frustration, she walked to the closet, forcing his scent and image from her mind. She had to get a hold of herself. In a few hours she'd be at work, and she needed to be able to focus. Things were a lot more hectic during the day shift.

She perused the closet, searching for the perfect outfit for the day. She chose red, a color she didn't often wear, but red seem to fit the mood she was in. She had no intention of sulking because he'd disappeared without a word.

Daniel Buchanan was in for a big surprise. He made a mistake by messing with Renée Walker.

Chapter 7

The days passed and Daniel didn't call. She waited each night for the phone to ring, but it didn't happen. She'd gone through the entire range of emotions possible, but today, Sunday morning, she had reached a state of resignation.

He'd not been to the hospital and Jamie had asked for him on more than one occasion. By the end of the week, Jamie, too, had reached indifference. Renée could see it each time she visited the teenager.

What hurt most was that she'd given herself to him without reservations and he had, in a very callous, unfeeling way, rejected her.

Ironically, even though she'd being trying to talk herself out of a relationship, she still wanted him. She knew Daniel had to be dealing with issues about his wife or work, but it did not lessen the hurt she was feeling. They needed to talk. Maybe, just maybe, they'd rushed into the lovemaking too soon.

She couldn't wait any longer. She needed to talk to him. She searched for her cell phone and quickly found his number, but again, the only response she got was his deep baritone over the voice mail.

At that moment, she made up her mind. She wasn't going to call him again. If they were going to talk, he'd have to do the calling. She'd left enough messages and was beginning to sound like the whining, dumped girlfriend. And she was not that kind of woman.

She was concerned about him. She couldn't help the hurt or pain that burned inside at the thought of his suffering. He'd lost everything that was important to him.

The ding of the toaster oven drew her from her thought. Good. She'd eat breakfast and face the day head on. If Daniel decided to call her, then that was his choice. If he didn't that, too, was his choice.

Life was all about choices. She, too, had a choice, and she had all intentions of fulfilling her promise. What she needed to do was make sure that she protected her heart and not lose it again. She'd done the love thing already and didn't want to go there once more. She had to put things in perspective and make sure that she remained in control. That was the word: *control.*

She'd always prided herself on her ability to be in control of any situation; something that worked well for her in her job. But when she loved, she knew she loved deeply, very deeply.

The phone rang and she jumped, almost screaming out. She glanced at the display before she answered it: the hospital. She picked the phone up.

"Hello?"

"Hi, Renée, it's Cheryl. Sorry to disturb you on your off day. But I needed to talk to you about something important.

With relief, Renée settled down. "Cheryl, you know it's not a problem."

"I knew you'd say that. It's about Jamie. She's asking to be released, but I know you wanted to talk to her before she left. I can hold her for another twenty-four hours but that's all."

"I plan on calling Gloria today to find out if she has room for one more. Of course, we'll have to find out if Jamie is willing to go," Renée assured her.

"I could talk to her since that's where I grew up. If not for Gloria taking me in as a foster child, I may have ended up on the streets, too. She took care of me for five years. I owe her my life."

"I'll call Gloria and let her know. I'll come see Jamie as soon as I get there tomorrow morning," Renée added.

"I hope you're enjoying your day off. Don't forget we're meeting tomorrow night for drinks."

"Of course, I haven't forgotten. Are Paula and Denise coming?"

"Yeah, Denise is back from the cruise and raving about it. She said she hasn't heard from you. You haven't returned any of her calls."

"I know she called, but I haven't actually checked my messages in days," Renée replied.

"I know you and those messages. I'm tired of telling you, you need to return your calls."

"I promise I'll check them as soon as I put the phone down. And I'll give Denise a call."

"Good, and I'll see you tomorrow night."

"Definitely."

Renée put the phone down. She really needed to do better. She often got so busy she forgot all about her friends. No wonder she always felt lonely. It was these same friends who'd been there for her when she'd found herself jilted. Maybe spending more time with her friends would keep her mind off of Daniel.

But she couldn't help but worry about what had become of him. He'd just disappeared off the face of the earth. She hoped it had nothing to do with what had happened between them.

She picked up the phone and dialed Denise's number. Denise's cheerful voice came on the line. Good, for a few moments, she could forget about Daniel Buchanan.

Daniel instinctively knew that the caller was Renée. The day after he'd spent the night at Renée's, he'd called his boss and told him he needed some personal time. Fortunately, he had a few weeks of vacation time saved up. He'd packed a bag with a few shirts, a couple of pants and some underwear, and got in his car and drove to New York. He'd stayed at a hotel in Manhattan, taken in a few shows, and spent the rest of his time watching television, reading, sleeping and eating.

Of course, he'd also spent some of the time thinking. Actually it was more like he had spent most of the time thinking about his life…and about *her.*

He had not been able to get her off his mind.

But now, after what he'd done to Renée, that unforgiving individual he had once been had resurfaced, and the cruelty of what he'd done ripped at his stomach.

Tonight, he would call her. No, he would go over to her apartment and tell her the whole story. He owed her that much. Maybe she would be willing to forgive him if she realized that he was being man enough to say he was sorry.

He picked up the phone and called the florist whose shop was just up the road.

A single rose and a note…*Forgive me.* Hopefully, he was doing enough.

Inside his mind was in turmoil, but there were things he had to exorcise if he was going to be happy.

He knew now that in order to be happy he would have to reveal his very soul.

Chapter 8

Forgive me.

The words were simple and clear. She was still upset that he had totally ignored her for the past week, but this single rose seemed to be working its charm. Or should she say, he was working *his* charm.

She couldn't believe she had fallen so easily for what he'd offered. She had exposed herself and knowing what happened between them had been more than just sex only made her feel more exposed.

Why did Daniel have to come into her life at this time? She had been slowly, very slowly, building up to the kind of life she wanted.

She was happy with her job. She had great friends. Okay, she didn't spend as much time with them as she should, or could, but they were great friends. And she had a home.

She had fallen in love with the apartment from the moment she'd seen it and had given the agent the sale immediately. She'd spend her first month there furnishing it and since then had added her own personal touches with a flair she didn't realize she had.

The rooms, painted in a bone white and trimmed with leather brown, were spacious and roomy. Afro-American and Caribbean art she purchased hung from every wall, adding vibrant color to the spare palette. The furniture, all mahogany, was modern and classy.

She smiled, experiencing a surge of pride at what she'd accomplished. She'd created a place of her own. She'd created a home.

Forgive me.

She glanced at the note again.

She hadn't expected it. She expected him to wallow in his self-pity again, and not come back up for air. Maybe this was another indication that he was on his way to healing. Maybe she needed to be around.

She didn't think she'd ever stop being amazed that he was a minister. He oozed sex appeal and his body was that of an African warrior…firm and strong. Her body still ached for him and often, at night, alone and cold, she'd brought thoughts of him into her bed and welcomed him with a fervor that almost felt real. His musky scent with a hint of his woodsy cologne still lingered.

What was she going to do?

There was a knock on her door. She wondered who

it was? Cheryl would usually call. Denise? No, she was at work.

She headed for the door and peered through the peephole.

Daniel.

She breathed deeply and then opened the door.

Her next thought was how fine he looked. Then an image of him naked and sweaty flashed in her mind. She realized that her resolution not to call him would be harder than she expected.

"How can I help you?" she said coldly.

He took a step backward before he said, "I believe I deserve that."

"You deserve that and more," she replied. She folded her arms across her chest and glared at him.

"I need to speak with you."

"I'm busy right now."

"It doesn't have to be now. Whenever you're available."

When she hesitated, he continued. "I know I'm the last person you want to talk to right now, but we need to talk."

"Since it's so important to you, I suppose I can spare a few minutes now," she said begrudgingly and stepped aside, confirmation that he could enter.

He walked into the room and she could tell he was uncomfortable. She closed the door and followed him inside. When he turned, he smiled shyly and her heart melted. Her anger shattered into tiny fragments. She couldn't help but return the smile. She could tell it had taken all of his courage to come there tonight. She willed the social worker inside her to surface.

She indicated the couch and, when he sat, moved to the chair adjacent to where he was sitting. For a moment there was silence and then he spoke.

"I was in New York."

She didn't respond. She'd give him time to say what he wanted.

"I'm sorry. I know it's almost midnight, but I wanted to talk to you before I went home. I'm not sure how to say what I have to say, so maybe, it's best to begin at the beginning."

"That's fine," she responded.

"Three years ago, my wife and daughter died in a car accident. I was at home working on my sermon. I was supposed to go to the store. I didn't and my wife went instead. A drunk driver slammed into the car. They both died instantly." His voice was low, dull, as if he were trying to keep his emotions under control. She ached to take him in her arms but she knew he needed to talk.

"I died along with them that night. For the first time in my life, I couldn't talk to God. Everything I'd worked so hard to establish just seemed like a joke. I'd dedicated most of my life to people and this was what God had done to me. Can you imagine putting your wife and your child into the ground at the same time? Sometimes at night, I still see that small, white coffin, and I get so angry."

"So you blamed God," she said.

"Yes, a part of me did. And a part of me blamed

myself. But I thought that God would have made an exception for me. He didn't."

"I'm sure He understood your anger at the time," she said, her tone reassuring him.

"Yes, I'm sure He did," he said with resignation. "But I couldn't deal with it. So I just packed my bags and left. I just wanted to get away from everything. My home, my family... I couldn't bear how they looked at me; as if I were some pathetic fool."

"I'm sure they were just concerned."

"I know, but at the time, I felt like I hated everyone. I'd already lost a brother, and then my father. I couldn't deal with it, so I lashed out at God. It was the easiest thing to do."

"So what did you do?" she asked gently.

"That's when I left. I just left everything behind and haven't looked back since."

"So you've had no contact with your family whatsoever?"

He hung his head. "No, I haven't spoken to anyone in the past three years. I just couldn't deal with family or friends. Every day I miss them, but I'm still not sure I'm ready to go back."

"But that's what family is there for. To help you during these times."

"You didn't know the Daniel I was back then. I will be the first to admit that I've changed drastically. I fooled people, had them eating out of my hand. I was quick to condemn those that did wrong and the congregation loved it. I was even quick to condemn my brother Corey because he was gay. And even more so when he committed suicide." He paused for a moment. She saw the glistening of tears in his eyes. He wiped them away, bringing himself under control.

"But I was filled with pride. I loved the power that I had. There was a part of me that felt as if I were a god. So when my wife and daughter died, I felt powerless. I didn't want God in my life anymore. But I've resolved my conflict with Him. I let Him stay where He is and He leaves me alone."

"That seems a bit extreme," she responded and then immediately regretted her words. She saw the veil that hid his thoughts and emotions.

For a while, there was silence, but then he spoke again. "That's why I went to New York. I had to get away. I couldn't deal with my feelings for you. But while I was there, I realized that I always do that. I run away from things I don't want to handle. I've always taken the easy way out."

"But you came back." She pulled her chair closer to his and reached out to hold his hands.

"I'm sorry about your wife and daughter. I deal with death daily at the hospital, but it's still hard for me to understand you leaving your family."

"I've had to deal with many deaths in my family in recent years. My brother Corey, my dad, and then Lorraine and Chelsea. Death hasn't been easy on my family."

"But you're still alive. You have other brothers?"

"Yeah, three."

"Three?" she echoed.

"Patrick, Taurean and Mason. Corey, my youngest, died several years ago."

"I'm sorry to hear that."

"It's fine. It's a long time ago. The good memories are there. Corey was special. It took me a long time to realize that." His voice cracked, thick with emotion.

He reached for her, coaxing her to sit next to him on the couch.

"Now I've definitely talked a bit too much about me. I'd like to hear some more about you. What made you the strong, confident woman you are."

"I like it better when you were doing all the talking," Renée said with a tender smile.

He gave a short laugh. "I know, but all that emotional chitchat has left me drained."

"Well," Renée started, "I've always had a good family life, though my father died when I was young. My mother has always been supportive. A bit too much at times. Then I met Cheryl and her foster mother Gloria. Gloria was the best. She encouraged us to dream big. I've made arrangements for Jamie to go live with her, actually."

"That would be a great idea. She needs to have some sense of family. Most of these runaways are kids who just want to be loved."

"Well, Gloria has lots of that to give. She was there to help me when I almost got married a few years ago and my groom never turned up at the church. My mother did warn me about him, but I didn't listen."

After a moment of quiet, he spoke. "Seems that both of us have had our share of heartache."

"Yeah, I'm sure we all have to deal with something drastic in our lives." She paused and then continued. "I know I shouldn't ask this, but are you planning to connect with your family?"

Daniel was silent for a while. "To be honest, I'm not sure. They've probably all moved on with their lives. Patrick and Taurean are married. And my other brother Mason got married a few weeks after my wife and daughter died."

"They must be worried about you."

"I'm sure they aren't. My brothers may love me, but they merely tolerated me when I was at home. When my brother Taurean went to prison, I refused to go see him. When he came out and visited us, he forgave me without hesitation. He's one of the most noble people I know. Me? I'm just a reject that God threw out. I was full of pride and self-righteousness. They're better off without me."

"I'm sure they don't feel that way, not if they really love you."

He hesitated before he responded. "Maybe what you say is true. But I'm not ready to deal with them yet."

"Well, you can't run away from them forever," Renée added before Daniel became silent.

"I think it's about time I go," he said finally. "I have work early in the morning. I'll think about what you said," he replied sincerely.

"I'm sorry. I didn't mean to upset you," she said.

"I'm fine. Just a bit tired. I took a late flight. I don't mean to seem closed off. I'm taking this in baby steps. I suppose I'm on the proverbial road to healing. I'm not sure. But I'm doing it in my own time and at my own pace."

"I understand. I agree. You should be getting home. You do look tired. And you must come in and see Jamie. She's been asking for you."

"I will. Thanks for listening to me. I really think I need someone to talk to."

"I'm glad I could help."

With that, he turned and headed for the door. She followed.

He stopped suddenly and glanced at a painting on the wall.

"What is it?" she asked.

"That painting? Whose work is it?" Daniel asked.

"Alana Buchanan," she replied, then paused, her eyes widening. "Buchanan."

He laughed. "That's Taurean's wife. I'd know her work anywhere. It's been here all this time?"

"No, I only hung it recently. A friend of mine bought it for me while she was on vacation. I love it."

"Yes, Alana is very talented." He turned to her. "I have to go. It's getting late."

He walked to the door and opened it. But then he turned around and pulled her to him. Her arms instinctively wrapped around him and they kissed. Despite their anger and frustration, the kiss was a gentle touching of lips, a lingering of tongue on tongue. His desire was evident and he began to kiss her hungrily, almost as if he were desperate. But then he pulled away suddenly, leaving her aching for more.

For a moment they stared at each other and then he broke the silence.

"Now I should really go. Have a good night." He turned and walked away, leaving her with a feeling of emptiness that she was growing accustomed to when he was not around.

Renée closed the door and headed straight for the bedroom. She flung herself on the bed and, without warning, tears sprung from her eyes. She cried for Daniel. For the hurt and pain she knew he was experiencing. She cried for her own loneliness and the fact that she needed him.

When she could cry no more, she pulled the covers closer, snuggled into the fluffy pillows she loved and fell asleep, only to dream of a tall, handsome prince who'd come and kiss her hurt away.

And in her dream the prince had the most beautiful amber eyes.

Daniel slowed the car and parked it in the brightly lit parking lot. He stepped out, heading to the tiny pond in the middle of the gardens near his home. He'd discovered the place by chance, but it was here he came when he needed to think, and tonight he needed to think.

Tonight had gone well. He'd finally opened up to Renée. He'd wanted to spend the night with her, but he needed to be by himself. Tomorrow he'd start to approach life with a different attitude.

What Renée had said to him about his family was true. He loved his family and knew he had the capacity to love again. Strangely enough, with his wife, he had been a totally different person. He'd been devoted to her; and he would have done anything for her. When he discovered that she was pregnant, he was like a kid. He had been so excited, Lorraine had to plead with him to control himself.

Lorraine. There was a part of him which still loved her, but he knew that he needed to let go, and until he could, he would never find happiness with someone else.

Did he want happiness?

For years he'd never thought of someone in the way he thought of Renée. She was so unlike Lorraine. While Lorraine had been a lady, she'd focused so much on being the perfect minister's wife that at times she'd almost seemed mechanical, as if she were acting out some spiritual drama.

But she had loved him. He had felt it from the first time she'd walked up to him at church and invited him out. She had been bold and daring like that.

A bird screeched and the trees rustled with the gush of a strong wind. And then there was absolute silence. No wind, no birds, no cars in the distance. He was at one with the night and the silence. And in that moment, he finally accepted that he needed to face all aspects of his life head on. He'd stopped running physically, but emotionally he was still avoiding facing the issues that hindered his healing. He had lived his life in the past, sitting in the judgment seat. In church, he had preached the Word of God. He had admonished his congregation to live by the principles of Christianity: fear of God, forgiveness, charity and brotherly love.

But he had fallen short. He hadn't supported Taurean during his incarceration; he had felt that as the perfect pastor, he couldn't condone what Taurean had done. He had scorned Corey because of the disease he had contracted and spurred him most at the time when he needed love. Yes, he had failed, failed as a brother.

When Lorraine and his daughter had been taken away, he'd run away and he was still running. Instead of staying with the people who loved him and Lorraine, he had run away and left them to face their grief alone. He'd been the person he'd always been; he had thought only of himself. He knew now what he needed to do, but he still wasn't ready.

He inhaled deeply. He was going to be all right. Tonight, he'd made a step in the right direction. Tonight, he had started his healing. But his healing wouldn't be complete until he told his wife goodbye and dealt with the alienation from his family. Someday soon, he would make that move. Tonight, he had to do some thinking. Despite what he knew he had to do, he had no intentions of rushing into anything.

Of course, Renée was another complication, one that left him confused and flustered. He was attracted to her and there was nothing he could do about it. His guilt at times threatened to consume him. However, his connection to Renée was more than mere attraction. He liked her, really liked her. She was sexy and intelligent. She made him laugh and she cared about people. Those qualities said so much about the kind of person she was. She would make any man a great wife, but he wasn't sure he was that man.

In the distance, a clock struck midnight. It was time to go home. He needed to get some rest. He'd thought about his life too much in the fast few weeks and he felt drained. While he welcomed the changes he was experiencing, his unemotional existence, up until now, had made life safer, easier to handle.

He stood and looked out at the dark sky. Because of Renée, he was determined to face life full on. He had no intention of losing the battle.

Suddenly, he remembered Jerome. He'd been so focused on himself, he'd forgotten the fourteen-year-old would be worried. Tomorrow he would call him and let him know he'd been out of town. He needed to apologize. Maybe that's where he needed to focus his energy right now.

Maybe it would help him to forget the soft flowery scent of Renée.

Renée clicked on the hyperlink and glanced at the picture of Alana Buchanan. She was amazed by how easy it was to find information on Daniel and his family. Fragments of information he'd mentioned in their conversation had sent her searching. She knew what she was doing was crazy, but she would not be happy unless she understood Daniel and his family.

She found information about Daniel's father's death, about the accident, which had killed his wife and child, and information about Alana Buchanan. It seemed that Taurean had married quite the famous artist, and fortunately there was a showing of her work in Chicago in a couple of weeks. Both Alana and her husband would be there.

She glanced at a photo of one of Alana's paintings and the vibrancy of the beautiful island of Barbados. Renée had never been there, but she'd seen enough of the island on television to know that it was a beautiful place. She then printed several articles on the family and powered off the computer.

She'd left an article from a newspaper to read last. It was an article written after the funeral of Daniel's wife and child. The photo accompanying the article focused on Daniel. He wore a black suit, but what she noticed most about him was his face. He was still handsome, but he looked haggard and devastated. He also looked angry. She could feel the anger emitting from the pages of the paper.

It was obvious Daniel still carried much anger inside. She wondered if she could help him deal with it. She knew she shouldn't interfere, all her good sense told her not to, but she had to do something. She'd call his brother, that's what she'd do. She'd call the hotel when she knew they were scheduled to be there.

No matter what Daniel thought, she knew that the only way he could heal completely was to resolve the conflict between himself and his family. He needed to love again—and it had to start with his family.

Renée lifted the papers from the printer's tray and carried them into the bedroom. She flopped onto the bed and started to read.

An hour later she was done. The articles had given her greater insight into the Buchanan family, and although there was not much about Daniel, she found the family fascinating.

Daniel's older brother Taurean had spent seven years in prison for euthanasia. His younger brother, Corey, had contracted AIDS and Taurean had helped to put him out of his suffering. Soon after Taurean's release from prison, their father had passed away. Daniel had married Lorraine Harvey and Taurean had married the then-unknown artist, Alana Smyth-Connell.

There was a photo of Daniel at the funeral of his dad and his appearance seemed so at conflict with the person he was now. Though he still rarely smiled, the stoic expression on his face reminded her of those fire and brimstone pastors, whose sole goal in life was to scare people away from hell. She could see what he meant when he told her about the person he'd been. The photo showed that man clearly. The Daniel she knew now was softer, kinder, and though his eyes hid his deeper feelings, the glimpses of gentleness she sometimes saw were definitely of a changed man.

Was she falling in love with him?

Love was a complicated feeling and one that often wreaked havoc. She wanted to approach this relationship—no, friendship—without any complications. And she needed to stick to her plan for the relationship. That's what she would tell Daniel. Let them be friends. Friendship was what each of them needed. Lovemaking brought too many other variables into what they had right now. Each of them had problems to resolve before they could be anything more to each other.

She needed to go to the store, pick up some groceries and come back to make some plans for tomorrow. Her obsession with Daniel Buchanan was making her lose focus on the important things in her life.

Chapter 9

Jerome dropped the basketball, turned and walked away. The other boys began to jeer, but he kept on walking. He glanced across at Daniel, the anger in his eyes like flares. Daniel felt his pain, but he knew he could not follow him. Jerome needed to work on his own self-control.

The practice session ended half an hour later and Daniel headed to his office. Jerome was standing outside. He assumed the boy had left the premises. He opened the door and invited Jerome to enter. Jerome followed, the scowl still on his face. Daniel indicated a chair and Jerome sat.

"You all right?" Daniel asked.

At first, Jerome didn't answer. "Man, I'm fine," he finally said.

"You're sure about that. You don't look fine to me."

"Okay, I'm angry, man. Those boys just piss me off at times. So I decided the best way to deal with it is to walk away. I don't have time for nonsense."

"That's good."

"Isn't that what you told me is the right thing to do?"

"You did it because you thought I expected you to behave that way?" Daniel said, leading him into further conversation.

"That's part of it. But I didn't want to get into any trouble this time. I'd be just like them if I did."

Daniel felt a surge of pride. He was making progress. In the past Jerome would have struck out in anger. A fight would have been inevitable.

"So you're learning to control that temper of yours."

Jerome looked at Daniel, a boyish grin on his face. "Yeah, I hear what you say. I don't want to be no thug. I got dreams, too. I don't have to stay down. That's what you told me."

"And how about your school work?"

"I'm still beating the books. Grades should be good this semester. I like getting A's."

Daniel nodded. "Good. Listen, I have some stuff I have to deal with here right now. I'll talk with you the next time you come."

"Cool, boss." Jerome got up and stopped before he left. "And…I just wanted to say thanks."

"For what?"

"For caring." Jerome replied, then walked out.

* * *

Renée jumped out of bed.

10:04 a.m.

Damn, she was late for work. And on a Monday. Work started at ten o'clock this morning. She checked the alarm and realized she had not set it. It was a nightly habit that she never forgot. Until last night. Last night, she'd fallen asleep.

She believed she and Daniel had made a step in the right direction. She wasn't sure where they would be going from here, but she planned on taking steps. He was a good man. An honorable man. She didn't know the person he'd been, but the Daniel she saw now was a man any woman would be proud to have. But this was no time for reflecting.

She had so many things on her schedule. A meeting, a call to make about Jamie, a short meeting with Cheryl and the list went on. Now she could see that her day was going to be a long one, so instead of rushing to work she'd call in, let them know she'd be in late, and would work late, as she often did anyway.

An hour later she walked into the hospital, took the staff elevator, and walked down the corridor to her office.

Her assistant was there, back from vacation, and with a cheerful good morning she handed Renée a stack of letters as thick as a ream of paper.

"Sorry, I know that this is not your idea of how to start the morning."

"Thanks, Gillian, and welcome back. I hope you enjoyed your trip to the Caribbean?"

"Yes, Jamaica was great. Had me a hot little island romance."

They both laughed and Renée said, "Hold my calls for the next hour or so. I'll let you know when I'm ready."

"Will do," Gillian replied. The phone rang. Using this as her opportunity to get away, Renée headed for her office.

She liked Gillian. She was hardworking and knew how to do her job. They worked well together.

Entering her office, she headed straight for her desk and sat down, slipping her heels off and slipping into the comfortable pumps she kept under her desk.

Her cell phone rang. She glanced at the caller ID. Cheryl. She answered.

"Hi, Cheryl, what's up?"

"Renée, I know you just got in but I need you to come and see Jamie. She's being discharged today. She's not talking to anyone. She says she won't talk to anyone but you or Daniel."

"I'll be there. I have to make some plans for her before her checkout time. I'll just make a few calls. I'll be down in about twenty minutes."

"Okay, I'll meet you in her room. She's giving the nurses a hard time."

"Just let her know I'm coming."

"I'll see you then," Cheryl said before breaking the connection.

Renée made the call to Gloria to let her know that Jamie would be arriving that day. Gloria had been excited at the prospect of having a new charge to care for. Renée could not understand how the old lady had so much room in her heart to love another child. If there was anyone who could show Jamie love, it'd be Gloria.

Renée left her office, informing Gillian where she was going. She heard Jamie before she reached her room. The teenager was screaming at the top of her lungs. She hurried down the corridor. Damage control was necessary.

When she entered the room, she was sure that her shock registered. Food lay scattered on the floor along with a puddle of whatever beverage the girl had been given. However, the rest of Jamie's midday meal dripped slowly down the front of Cheryl's white blouse.

The look on Cheryl's face was incredulous, but Renée knew better than to laugh. She felt proud of Cheryl, since it had taken her a long time to control her anger. Her current calm was clear evidence of her ability to remain calm, despite the anger Renée knew bubbled beneath the surface.

"Jamie." Renée called her name.

The teenager turned and Renée's heart almost broke. She could see the tears of anger in Jamie's eyes.

"Cheryl, I'll take over from here. Give us some time."

"Okay, we'll talk later. I'll send someone in later to clean up the room up."

When Cheryl was gone, Renée moved closer. Jamie had stopped crying, her head was on the pillow and she was staring at Renée, stiff with defiance.

"So what's the problem, Jamie?"

"Nuttin'."

"I'm sure if the problem was nothing, you'd have just eaten your lunch without incident."

"I have nothing to say."

"Jamie, do you trust me?"

"No, I don't trust anyone," she said between sniffles.

"So why did you ask for me?"

"'Cause you're the only one in this smelly place who ain't a fraud."

"That's good to know. But if I'm not a fraud, why don't you trust me?"

"You tryin' to confuse me or something?" Jamie asked.

"No, just asking a simple question," Renée responded.

"Okay, I think I trust you, but you better not be playing with me."

Renée moved closer to the bed. She reached out and held Jamie's hands.

"You can trust me, Jamie. I just want the best for you. I promise I won't do anything without your knowing. And that's one of the reasons I'm here. I've found a home for you."

"I ain't going anywhere I'm not wanted."

"I promise you, you have nothing to worry about. The lady who you're going to stay with is Gloria. She was Cheryl's foster mother. You'll like her. There will be a few other girls there. If you don't like it there, I'll make sure I find somewhere else where you can go."

"You don't have to put yourself through so much trouble. Just let me go where I was. I can take care of myself."

"Okay, I'll make you a promise. If you don't like being with Gloria, I'll let you do whatever you want to."

It seemed like minutes passed before Jamie spoke. "I'll go," she said reluctantly. "But I'm going to hold you to your promise."

"Good. I'll take you over there when you've been discharged. The doctor should be here soon. I have to go up to my office for a little bit. I'll come down as soon as Dr. Archer arrives. You can get dressed after he leaves."

Renée reached out to touch Jamie's hand. They were trembling. Renée looked at her and realized something. She was still a little girl. Under all that boldness and bravado, she was just a little girl looking for love. Renée felt the urge to hug her, but she decided against it. Gloria's home would be the ideal place. Jamie would get all the hugs she wanted.

"I'll be back," she said softly. Jamie smiled in return, and resting her head back against the pillows, closed her eyes.

Renée turned and left the room. She'd call Gloria and let her know that she would be dropping by later. She stepped out into the corridor and came face-to-face with Daniel. She could tell he was trying to remain calm, but she noticed the signs that he was uncomfortable. She smiled, a smile she knew didn't reach her eyes. She was still annoyed with him, and waiting patiently to see what he had to say.

"Hi," was the only thing he said.

She responded likewise. She tried to think of

something witty to say, as women in movies would, but nothing came to mind.

Instead, she realized that sticking to business would be better.

"You've come to see Jamie?" she finally asked.

"I haven't seen her since I came back. I just wanted to know how she's doing."

"She's in her room. She'd being discharged today. I'll be taking her over to the lady I told you about."

"I hope she's all right with that."

"She promised me that she would give it a try."

"That's good. At least she's willing to give it a chance."

"You can go in and chat with her. I just need to go to my office to collect her files and I'll be back."

"We have to talk," he replied.

All she could do was nod. She knew that they'd have to talk. She wasn't looking forward to it, but it was definitely inevitable.

She turned and walked away, refusing to look back. She could feel his eyes looking through her. Heat coursed through her body and when she stepped into the elevator she sighed in relief. Seeing Daniel always seemed to leave her disoriented…and flushed.

When she reached her office, she sat and searched for the papers she needed and then she stared at the clock, watching the hand move slowly along.

A half hour later, her phone rang and she snatched it up. It was Cheryl. Dr. Archer had come and gone. She put her things away, fixed her desk and headed back downstairs.

When she reached the room, she heard laughter coming from inside. It was husky male laughter and the delightful giggle of a teenage girl. Inside the picture was one she'd longed to see. Laughter transformed Jamie. She positively sparkled, and Renée almost cried with relief. Her eyes moved to Daniel. He hadn't seen her enter. He, too, had been transformed. He seemed more relaxed, more carefree.

This was the man she was falling in love with. Each aspect of his personality fascinated her, warmed her until she wanted to hold him and never let go.

He turned and their eyes met.

"Daniel has offered to take you and Jamie to Gloria's house. I accepted for you," Cheryl said. She'd changed her blouse.

The look on Renée's face was incredulous and Daniel did all he could to control his laughter. She didn't want to be around him, but he had offered for a reason. He had to talk to her. To apologize. He realized he had been insensitive and unkind. He needed to rectify the situation. He wanted them to be friends. He wanted them to be more, but he didn't want to get much closer yet. His family situation still needed to be resolved. But he didn't want her to intrude in that part of his life. Next she would start acting like she was his counselor and helping him to deal with his troubled mind.

He knew that she didn't want to spend any more time than necessary with him, but he wanted to talk to her and would do anything possible to make sure they were alone. Yet he couldn't *make* her talk. She was still angry at the way he had treated her. She couldn't help him if he kept trying to pushing her away.

He watched as Renée helped Jamie pack her bag, her back stiff and unbending. He knew her posture, her attempt to ignore him, was a cover for how she was really feeling.

She finally turned to him and said, "We're ready."

"Good, my car is in the parking lot. I'm going to get the car and drive around to the pickup point. You can bring Jamie down," he replied.

"Thank you. I hope we're not taking up too much of your time."

"Of course not. I've finished work for the day. I'm all yours," he replied, the smile on his face expanding.

She ignored him again and helped Jamie from the bed into a wheelchair.

He exited the room, holding the door open for them. When they started down the corridor he quickened his step. "I'll go ahead. Just wait for me outside."

He turned and walked away, smiling as he did. He'd really got under her skin today and he was having so much fun with her discomfort. He walked quickly down the stairs to the bottom floor and took the exit that led directly to the parking lot. In a few minutes he was pulling up at the main entrance where Renée and Jamie stood waiting.

He stopped the car, stepping out and opening the door for each of them. When Jamie was seated in the backseat, he helped Renée in and she stepped inside. Their hands touched and he felt the now familiar spark of awareness their physical contact resulted in. She pulled her hands away and he looked at her, willing her to lift her head. She did, and he saw the flames burning in her eyes.

She averted her gaze as he closed the door, before he rounded the car and got in. Again there was that moment of intensity when his leg touched hers. She shifted hers, moving her body closer to the door.

He pulled out of the driveway and made his way onto the highway. The drive was uneventful. When he realized that she had no intention of talking, he turned the radio on and let it do the speaking.

It took twenty minutes to reach Gloria's home, the sterile concrete of the city soon giving way to residential suburbs. Tall trees lined the streets, children played on the sidewalks.

When Renée indicated an open gate, he pulled in and drove slowly down the wide driveway. The gardens were magnificent, with well-tended hedges and rows and rows of flowers.

From the backseat, he heard Jamie's cry of surprise. "Wow, this lady must be loaded. What would she want with delinquent children like me?"

"Oh, she'll tell you her whole story before the end of the day, I'm sure," Renée said.

Jamie did not respond. Instead, like Daniel, she stared at the massive colonial mansion they'd driven up to. Daniel parked the car and waited, unsure of what to do.

"You can park the car over there," Renée instructed.

Daniel followed her instruction and parked the car

next to a new BMW, the kind of car he dreamed of as a child. He got out and headed to the back where he helped Jamie out of the car.

Renée watched him. Ever gentle, he took Jamie's bag making sure she was fine before he followed them toward the house and up the marble steps. Before they reached the door a well-dressed, older woman stepped out.

Not in keeping with the ladylike image, she screamed at the top of her lungs and opened her arms to embrace Renée.

"Renée, it's so good to see you. You haven't been by in ages. I was getting ready to send the cavalry out."

"I'm sorry. I've been so busy the past few weeks. But I'm here now."

"So this is the young gentleman who's been keeping you so busy," Gloria said, her gaze focused on Daniel.

"No," Renée responded quickly. "He's just a colleague who's working on a case with me."

"It's nice to meet you, *colleague,*" she replied. "I'm Gloria. And since Renée hasn't given me a name, the honor is yours."

"Daniel Buchanan. I'm a counselor at The Hope Center. Renée and I have been working with this fine young lady here together."

"Oh, that's wonderful. I had a child from Hope Center before. You do good work for children." She turned to Jamie. "And this beautiful young lady must be Jamie. Welcome to my home."

Jamie smiled shyly.

"I'll get Delores to take you up to your room and introduce you to the other girls," Gloria continued.

The young girl who was standing at the door stepped forward and took Jamie's bag.

"Hi, I'm Delores," she said to Jamie. "The other girls can't wait to meet you."

Daniel noticed that Jamie relaxed physically. She was going to be fine. There was just something about this place that spoke of love and security. He was glad Renée thought about placing her here.

"I like what you're doing here for the girls."

"Oh, Daniel Buchanan, it's my life. Someone has to help save these girls. Somebody helped and saved me. I have no choice but to do my part. God saw it fit to bless me after a bad start in the world. He deserved no less from me."

"I wish everyone in the world thought like you do. Maybe the world would be a better place."

"Isn't that the truth. Now, would you like to come in to have a cup of coffee or tea?" Gloria asked.

Before Renée could respond, Daniel answered. "I'm sorry. Renée and I have some business to discuss. And I've learned that it's best when introducing a child to a new situation that it's best to let them discover things and meet people on their own."

He could tell from the look on Renée's face that she was not happy. He was sorry he had to do this, but they needed to talk before their already fragile relationship deteriorated any more. Plus, he wanted to make sure Jamie really did get a chance to bond with the other girls without their interference.

Daniel watched as Renée took Gloria in her arms and hugged her tightly.

"I love you," she told her old friend.

"Love you, too," Gloria replied. They moved apart and Gloria turned to him.

"It was nice meeting you, young man. You take care of my Renée and be sure to come back and see me. I'm sure we'll have a lot to talk about."

Gloria paused for a moment. "I think I'm going to like you, Daniel." She turned to Renée. "You take care of him and don't let him get away."

Renée blushed and looked uncomfortable, but she did not respond, only smiled.

"Well, enjoy the rest of the evening. I'm going in to have a chat with Jamie. And don't be a stranger." With that, she turned and walked in the direction they'd taken Jamie.

Minutes later, Daniel drove out into the busy downtown street. He turned to Renée. "Want to get something to eat? We can talk, as well."

She nodded. "That's fine."

"My apartment or yours?" he asked cautiously.

"I'd prefer mine. I have a lot of work to do at home."

"Renée, I know you're still annoyed with me, but we need to talk. If after we talk you want to go your merry way, then that's what will happen. Is that fine with you?"

He could feel her eyes on him, long and hard.

"Okay, I'll go with you. And we'll *talk*." She made a point to emphasize the word.

They rode in silence, both troubled by their individual thoughts. Tonight they'd talk and that was all. For him, it would be difficult, especially with that dress Renée wore that highlighted her curves. He had no intention of letting its subtle seductiveness tempt him. He planned to be on his best behavior.

Tonight he planned on sleeping in his own bed, alone.

The dinner sparked with tension. Renée wondered how this was all going to end. A large bucket of extra crispy chicken, biscuits, mashed potatoes and gravy, were spread out on the table on the balcony, which provided a view of the city that was made for romance. Autumn was in the air, but it was not chilly enough to remain indoors. In fact, the slight chill only served to invigorate.

Daniel placed an unfinished chicken breast on the plate, rubbed his stomach and sighed with contentment.

"I must admit, I love this chicken and there is nothing like these biscuits."

"I know what you mean. I try to avoid junk food, but there is just something about the Colonel."

She bit another piece of the chicken and placed her fork on the plate. "I can't eat another bite."

He wiped his mouth. "So, can we have our little talk now?"

"Yes, that's fine," Renée replied.

"I just wanted to say how sorry I was about the other night. The attitude and all," he said.

"It doesn't matter," she replied.

"You know that's not true, Renée. I can't continue this conversation if we can't be honest with each other." He paused for a moment. "Look. I like you. You're the first woman I've had any interest in since my wife died. I'd like to explore what we have. I've been thinking about you all the time. I mean, the sex is great, but I want what we have to be much more."

"I know what you mean," Renée replied. "I like you, too. But what I don't want to feel is that I'm a substitute for your wife. Or that you're going to feel guilty each time we make love."

He nodded. "I promise you. It won't be about my wife. I'm dealing with that. I did feel guilty at first, but one of the things my wife made me promise when we first got married is that we were to make sure that we were both happy no matter what, whether we were together or not."

Renée continued to look him in the eyes.

"I'm not sure if I'm ready for serious commitment yet," he continued. "But I know that I want you and I want to be with you."

"I'd like that," she said softly. "That's how I feel, too. But I'm not sure I have the time to be in a serious relationship right now."

She stopped talking and reached across to him. She wanted to kiss him. Had wanted to all day, but she'd kept her need under control. Giving in to the craving would be to admit that she was weakening.

He kissed her, cautiously at first. But soon the kiss

deepened, his tongue slipping inside her mouth, teasing her and causing her to moan softly. Her hands reached out to grip him, drawing him even closer. She wanted to feel him against her. She shifted, indicating that they should move inside. He complied, picking her up and carrying her back inside, then putting her on the couch and climbing on top.

The kissing continued the entire time, and she wanted it to continue, to never stop. With every probe of his tongue, she felt shivers run along her spine and the ache and yearn of the heated spot between her legs. She could feel the force of his erection against her. The pulsing and the occasional jerk only served to increase her excitement. She wanted him inside her and though she knew she'd be making a mistake, she allowed her body to succumb to the desire.

The kiss deepened until the heat inside was too much to bear. She felt hot all over, and arched her body against his, wanting the physical contact that could give some relief to her boiling need. Renée placed her hand between his legs, gripping the proof of his desire. She eased him off of her, forcing him to stand between her legs, unbuttoning his jeans and letting them fall to the floor. His boxers followed, exposing his impressive erection. She wanted to pleasure him, to taste him.

She placed her mouth on him, delighted when his penis jerked lightly. His body tensed when she took him deeper inside her mouth, using her tongue to tease him, until his legs started to tremble with his excitement.

She stopped, wanting to take things even further.

Standing, she took her dress off and tossed it on a nearby chair. Then Daniel took control.

He lifted her, carrying her toward the desk in the corner of the room. He swiped the books on it onto the floor and sat her down, legs opened. He slipped a condom on and spread her legs wider, entering her.

The force of his entry surprised her, but she welcomed him with a wild animal cry. She curled her legs around his buttocks until she could feel the full length of his penis throbbing inside her.

Daniel thrusted into her hard, and she took each thrust with her own gyration. She placed her hands behind his back, feeling the firmness and force of his movement. She wanted to urge him on with words, but the only sounds she could make were cries of pleasure that made him move faster and thrust even deeper.

And when she thought she could take no more, her excitement intensified and white heat surged through her body. Her muscles clenched, and she screamed as spasm after spasm wracked her body. Seconds later, Daniel's body stiffened, and he growled as his penis contracted and jerked deep inside her, his body trembling powerfully with his own release.

Daniel held her tightly as they rode out the waves of their passion, until their breathing slowed and they regained some measure of control.

He kissed her again. A gentle, tender kiss that seemed so in contrast with what had just happened between them. While their tongues entwined, he lifted her tenderly and headed to the bedroom.

She wanted him again, but knew that they needed time to recover. She wasn't worried. She knew they'd make love again…and again…before the night was over.

Chapter 10

During the night, Daniel woke to the sound of gentle breathing. He looked down at the woman who'd fallen asleep in his arms. The moon cast a single ray of light which caressed Renée's face, making her appear even more beautiful. The contrast of light and shadows seemed in keeping with the nature of their relationship. However, he was sure that their relationship would move to another level after tonight.

Only three weeks and he was already falling in love with her. He didn't want to acknowledge the word, but there was nothing else that it could be.

Under the covers he hardened again. This woman had the ability to control him. She worked her magic and he loved it. He loved what she did to him and he loved what she made him do. The passion he shared with his first wife had been incredible, but with Renée things even went further.

Renée stirred and her eyes opened slowly. She smiled up at him.

"Thank you," she said.

"No, thank you," he responded.

"Mutual admiration," she said, laughter in her voice.

"I'm serious," he said. "I haven't felt like this in years. It's like a heavy weight has finally been lifted and I can breathe."

"It's healing," she replied. His fingers ran along her arm. She shivered. He knew how to arouse her.

"No, it's you," he repeated.

"Not really. I may have just come at the right time, but you were ready for this."

"At least I've made a start. Hopefully, I don't have too much further to go." His fingers had traveled upward and now trailed along one firm breast. "I know I need to make a trip back home to where Lorraine and Chelsea are buried. I need to say goodbye to them. I have to do that before I can move on."

"And what about the rest of your family? That's part of your healing. You won't be complete if you don't talk to them."

"I know how you feel about this, Renée, but I know my family. I'm not sure if I want to see them yet. They didn't even try to find me."

"But isn't that what you wanted? For them not to find you," she replied.

"I don't know. I may have wanted them to find me.

The past three years have been crazy years for me. Sometimes I'm not even sure what I wanted in that first year." She could hear the sadness in his voice and she ached for him.

"But your family is important."

"Let's not talk about my family anymore. I'll call them. Soon. But not now. I'm not ready."

Renée didn't reply. It wasn't that he didn't want to see his family. He did. But he was ashamed. He'd left them without one word…and maybe they were annoyed with him. He'd take his time…He'd get around to calling them. Maybe at Christmas. Or Thanksgiving. He knew he now had a lot to be thankful for.

His life was still a good one. He had a good job and even though he was no longer in the ministry, he made a difference. He'd loved counseling before the tragedy, but he loved his work now just as much.

He worked before to bring people to salvation. He'd been one of those ministers who called down fire and brimstone. His focus had been enforcing the rules, his rules. Today he offered them love, compassion and healing. That alone made him proud of what he did.

He drew nearer to Renée, placing his arms around her, her back curved into his stomach. She felt good next to him. He could see himself waking each morning with his arms around her. Fanciful thinking. Or was it? It was strange that even a few months ago he'd vowed that he would never marry again. But things had definitely changed. He'd changed. Now the future suddenly didn't look like a long, narrow, empty road. Tonight, the images he saw painted in the canvas of his imagination bloomed with flowers and vibrant color. And he owed it all to this beautiful, generous woman, who touched people's lives and had certainly touched his.

Her breathing slowed and soon she was fast asleep. Daniel stayed awake, thinking about her and how he'd changed long into the early morning hours and it was only when the sun peeked between the curtains that he finally fell into a quiet, untroubled sleep.

The next morning after Daniel left, Renée opened the paper to see Alana Buchanan, the artist, and her husband, Taurean, staring out at her. She immediately saw the resemblance. Daniel and Taurean could easily pass for twins, and only a discerning eye would be able to distinguish the subtle evidence of an age difference.

While Daniel's eyes concealed all his thoughts, Taurean's eyes sparkled with life, and from the way he was looking at his wife in the photo, Renée could tell he adored her. Renée's envy surprised her. But she knew why. She wanted that for herself. She wanted Daniel Buchanan to look at her with that same adoring, devoted look.

Renée read the article slowly. The show was scheduled for the next day at the Alan Koppel Gallery. She had to try to reach them. A part of her knew that she was intruding where she didn't belong, but she was encouraged by her need to help Daniel. He needed to be with his family and an opportunity like this couldn't be passed up. She knew he was going to be angry, but she could deal with him. She had to do this because she was thinking about him.

She picked the phone up and dialed the Marriott where they were staying. She asked to be connected to their room. "Hello," said a deep male voice, so similar to Daniel's.

"Hello, may I speak to Taurean Buchanan?" she asked.

"Yes, this is he."

"I'm sorry to call you at this time, Mr. Buchanan. I'm calling you about your brother, Daniel."

"Daniel? Who is this? This had better not be a joke!" Renée could tell he was annoyed.

She tried to calm him by reassuring him that the call was legitimate. As quickly as she could, she explained who she was and why she was calling.

Ten minutes later the call came to an end. Taurean had asked for Daniel's address. He promised he'd go there that night when Daniel was home. Renée hadn't expected things to move so quickly and experienced a slight feeling of dread.

Tomorrow, or later tonight, would tell how he would respond to her intrusion. She knew he'd be angry, but she was convinced she'd done the right thing.

Daniel stood, water cascading around him. He'd taken a well-deserved bath, and soaking himself within the soppy suds seemed to bring relief from a stressful day. Now that he was showering off, he thought back to the evening he had had.

Jerome had got into an altercation at school and had been sent home on suspension. The boy had refused to fight back, remembering that Daniel had told him how proud of him he was. Daniel was torn up when he'd rushed over to Jerome's grandmother's home. He had seen the tears in the boy's eyes. So much for the bravado Jerome tried so hard to show when the other boys were around. He kept saying, "See, I didn't fight back. I didn't fight back."

Daniel swelled with pride and only left the apartment when Jerome had finally fallen asleep. He promised he would return in the morning.

Now, he strolled out of the bathroom, drying his skin as he contemplated aimlessly.

The doorbell rang.

Damn, who could it be at this hour? he wondered. He wrapped the towel around him and rushed to the door. There was no one there. He eased the door open and peeped out, only to see a back that seemed familiar, but he couldn't place the person immediately.

The man turned around at the sound of the opening door.

Daniel's heartbeat accelerated.

Taurean.

He was at a loss for words.

Taurean hesitated for the briefest of moments, uncertainty scrawled across his face. Then he moved quickly, at a speed that belied his size. He wrapped his arms around Daniel, almost desperately. Daniel felt the moisture on his cheek and wondered if it was his brother's or his.

Never in his imagination had he expected his reconciliation with Taurean to be like this. He wondered how Taurean knew where to find him, but in time he'd find that out. Now, he just wanted to feel the comfort his brother's arms offered.

"I really think we should go inside before your neighbors get the wrong idea."

Daniel withdrew, glanced around, and they both laughed.

He placed his arm around his brother's shoulders and dragged him playfully into the apartment, closing the door behind them.

There was silence, as if after the show of affection they were both unsure of what to say.

"So, how are you doing, Daniel?" Taurean finally asked.

"I'm doing fine," he replied, his voice filled with emotion.

"You know I'm pretty angry with you."

"I suspected that much," Daniel said, knowing. "And you're still not worried about saying what's on your mind, I see."

"Yeah, one of those things we have in common," Taurean said, then paused. "You've changed," Taurean commented, "in a good way. You're not as stiff as you used to be. You're more relaxed, softer."

"Well, I can't argue with that. Come, sit down so we can talk. We have a lot of catching up to do."

"Give me a minute. I need to call Alana and let her know I found the place or else I'm sure my cell phone is going to ring soon."

Taurean pulled his BlackBerry out and made a quick call. Again, Daniel saw the spark of happiness in his eyes and heard the gentleness in his voice.

"Love you," were the last words he heard his brother say before he disconnected the call.

"Okay, Alana is a lot happier now. When I get back to the hotel we're going to call Melissa and Joanne."

"They must be a handful by now."

"Oh, yeah, both of them. Melissa is at one of the leading high schools on the island, The St. Michael School. And Joanne is just Joanne—smart, energetic and a handful."

"You don't need to say any more. If she has taken after any one of us, especially you, I can imagine."

They both laughed and then they were silent again.

"So when did you plan to call, to contact us? I was worried. I mean, it's been *three years*."

Daniel sighed. "I'm sorry, Taurean, but I needed to do what I did. Lorraine and Chelsea's deaths devastated me. I needed to save myself."

"I know, but I could have been there for you. You didn't let me," Taurean said.

"You mean like I should have been there for you? When I left, I hated myself. I hated the person I'd become. Now I look back, I didn't know how you all dealt with me. I was horrible."

"You were, but that doesn't mean we weren't worried. I was worried. A night hasn't passed when I haven't thought about you, wondered if you were all right. At least now I'll be able to get a comfortable night's sleep.

"I'm sorry," was all Daniel could say.

"Life for me has been wonderful. I have a beautiful wife who loves me and two of the greatest kids any man could want. But I need my brothers." He looked directly into Daniel's eyes. "Each one of my brothers."

"If it's any conciliation, I was planning to call some time soon."

"Well, I'm glad your girlfriend called."

"Girlfriend? Renée? Renée called?"

So she had done the calling.

"Yes, about an hour ago. She sounded worried about you. Is there something to worry about?" Taurean asked.

"No," he said quickly.

Taurean stared at him. "Okay, I'll trust you. If she would call me, she must be someone special. I know you, and you still can't lie to me."

"She's beautiful and I'm attracted to her but she confuses me."

"Sounds just the way I feel about Alana."

They laughed.

"So what are you doing in the Windy City?" Daniel asked.

"Alana is having a show at the Alan Koppel Gallery," Taurean replied.

"That's great. She must be doing really well to have an exhibition there."

"Oh, yeah. She makes more money on one painting than the resort does in months, and it isn't doing too badly, so that should give you an idea of the kind of money she commands."

"That's good. You must be so proud of her."

"I am. You have to come to the opening tomorrow

night…and bring your girlfriend. We'll go out to dinner afterward. Alana will be glad to see you."

Daniel hesitated.

"You can't *not* come," Taurean insisted. "Alana will be disappointed. I have no intention of losing you for another three years. I already lost you for those seven years I was in prison and your recent time in exile. You owe me."

"If you put it like that. I'll call Renée and let her know."

"Good. I wish I could stay longer, but I should really get back."

Taurean stood and Daniel followed suit.

"It's been good to see you, Bro. I missed you."

"I missed you, too," Daniel replied.

They gave each other one of those warm, brotherly hugs that had been so much a part of the Buchanan household.

"I love you, Bro," Taurean said. "We're going to talk. We have so much catching up to do. And you know Alana will be showing you all the photos of the kids tomorrow night."

"I look forward to seeing them. I didn't even ask how you got here."

"A hired car. Renée gave me the directions so it wasn't difficult to find the apartment building. I haven't been in Barbados that long, so I still remember the city."

When Taurean left, he picked up the phone and dialed Renée's number.

"Hi," she said timidly. "Everything okay?"

"Yes, everything's okay."

"You're not too angry with me, I hope?" she asked, uncertainty filling her voice.

"I should be angry, but I'm not," he reassured her. "I didn't realize that I wanted to see my family so much. Seeing Taurean makes things different. Of course I'm a little annoyed that you called them even though I told you not to, but my brother is my brother."

Relief was evident in her voice. "I'm glad things worked out okay. I'm sorry for calling but I knew I had to. I couldn't let him come here and you not see him."

"He invited me to the opening of the show tomorrow. You're invited, too. You can't refuse. Taurean is looking forward to meeting you."

"I'd love to join you," she responded.

Daniel heard a beep.

"Sorry, Daniel. I have to go," Renée said. "I'm expecting this call. I'll see you tomorrow. Bye."

Renée was right. She'd done what she'd done, but in the process she'd disregarded his wishes. He'd wanted to do things on his own time and she'd made the choice for him.

He did, however, understand her reason for doing what she did. Renée was so accustomed to helping people that she would think she had to help him. Daniel hoped this wasn't why she'd been so willing to spend time with him. That she saw him as some troubled, tragic hero who needed to be healed. A feeling of dread caused a physical pain in his gut. It immediately reminded him of when he'd lost his family.

He breathed in deeply. He had to take control of his life. He'd basked too long in the shadow of his past. Here he was again, blaming external forces for his state of mind when he was in control of who he was, who he'd become.

Maybe this was a new start for him.

Though he was off of work tomorrow, he planned on spending the day with Jerome. Here he was wallowing in his own despair and there was a young boy out there without a father or a friend. He had decided to do this work because he wanted to work with kids. He'd felt something for Jerome yesterday. He'd felt his heart cry out.

He enjoyed working with kids, always did, but since starting at the Center, he'd kept them at a distance—until Jerome. He didn't know why his thoughts were heading in that direction, but the boy needed a father. He was single and he was a counselor.

He'd spend some time with him and see where it went from there. Maybe it would keep his mind off of everything else that was going on. Tomorrow night he'd spend time with Taurean and his wife. Renée would be there.

Change. He'd always thought that change brought sadness with it. Instead, now he realized that change could bring something good.

Daniel finished eating his breakfast quickly and arrived at the Center just as the night shift was going off. He greeted his colleagues and explained that he knew it was his off day, but that he was in to do some work. He informed the counselor on duty that he wanted to see Jerome as soon as he arrived. He worked steadily on finishing the reports he needed to complete by month's end and was on the last one when there was a knock on his door.

"Come in," he said.

Jerome walked in, bedecked in his usual getup.

"Yo, man," he greeted Daniel.

"Yo," he responded.

"I heard you wanted to see me."

"What are your plans for the day?" Daniel asked him.

"Well, I was going to hang with my boys later and then I have this chick to meet."

"That means my plans can't work."

"What plans you mean, man?"

"I was going to ask you if you wanted to hang with me today."

"For real?" he asked and then stopped. "Man, it's cool. I can give my friends a call and let them know I'm going hang out with a friend. And I'm the man, I'll let the girl know, another time. She won't mind."

Daniel smiled. "So it's on then."

"Yeah, man. I can spare you a few hours of my valuable time."

"Okay, I'll be ready in about fifteen minutes. I just need to get this report completed."

"I'll go outside and hang until you're ready."

Jerome left the room, whistling. Daniel knew he'd made the right decision. He was sure Jerome didn't have any plans for the day, but his pride wouldn't allow him to admit it. In time, he hoped Jerome would learn to trust him.

* * *

Renée walked out of the changing room and turned around, striking a sensual pose.

"I totally approve," Cheryl exclaimed. "You're going to have him lusting after you all night."

"Okay, let me put it back. I want to look classy and elegant. I'm going to the opening of an art show. I don't want my date to feel like he's escorting someone without class."

"Renée, you know what I mean. You do look classy and elegant and *sexy*. The dress is perfect for the show. I'm not letting you leave unless you buy it."

"Okay, I do love it." Renée giggled. "You know me and red. But I'm going to be broke for the rest of the month."

Cheryl clapped. "You're going to be the belle of the ball—and you are getting to meet your brother-in-law to be."

"Cheryl, I think you're going a bit too fast." Renée laughed.

Her best friend laughed with her. Then she grabbed her hand and took her back to the dressing room. "We also need to get you some sexy undergarments."

"I don't need any!"

"Oh, yes, you do. I've seen what you have in those drawers." She giggled when she saw the look on Renée's face.

Renée couldn't help it, either, and broke down in a fit of laughter.

It would take Cheryl to cheer her up. She needed a

little boost of joy and Cheryl had a habit of knowing just what to do to get her smiling again.

They headed for the lingerie department after Renée paid for the dress. Of course, sexy was the aim, and Cheryl didn't relent. So they left the store with a shopping bag of Victoria's Secret panties and bras.

Tonight was going to be a good one. She had all intentions of enjoying the seduction.

Daniel watched as Jerome took photo after photo of the animals at the zoo. The boy was fascinated with animals. Daniel had been surprised when Jerome had said he wanted to go to the Brookfield Zoo, but he'd gone willingly. He'd expected the movies or an arcade. Of course, Jerome did stop to stare at a teenage girl who caught his eye. To say that Daniel was enjoying himself was an understatement. At fourteen, Jerome was smart and mature for his age.

"You ready to get something to eat?"

"I guess. But can we come back another day?"

"We're not leaving yet. Just getting a snack. But yes, we can come back, if you'd like. But you may not want to spend too many days with an old man like me."

Jerome didn't respond, but Daniel could tell he wanted to say something. He guessed that there were too many people around.

"What about I buy us burgers and fries and we sit on one of the benches over there," Daniel suggested.

"That's cool. Can I still watch the animals?" he asked.

"Sure," Daniel replied.

At that moment a man with his wife and two kids asked Daniel if he could take photos of them. After Daniel took several photos, the man turned to him and said, "I can see your son loves animals, too. My sons are just like yours. They would come here every week if I had the time. I try to bring them once or twice a month."

When the man and his family moved on, Daniel turned to Jerome who'd suddenly gone quiet. He just took the money Daniel gave him and went to buy the burgers and fries.

When Jerome returned, Daniel pointed to an empty bench. They ate in silence.

"So what's wrong, Jerome?" Daniel finally asked. "You've gone quiet on me."

"Sorry, I was just thinking."

"You want to share?" Daniel asked.

"It might make you angry," Jerome replied quietly.

"I promise I won't get angry. You haven't done anything to make me angry yet."

"I was just thinking about what that man said."

"What he said?"

"Yeah," he hesitated. "He thought you were my father."

"Yeah, he did."

"You didn't have a problem with it?" Jerome asked.

"No. I'd be proud of you if you were my son."

Jerome lowered his head. "If I told you I lied to you, you won't think so," Jerome said.

"I'm sure I won't change my mind."

"I told you this morning I was going out with my

friends and my girl. I don't have lots of friends. At least none that would invite me out. They all think I'm a thug, but I'm not. I just don't want anyone take advantage of me."

Daniel nodded.

"And you still want to hang with me. I guess I just… really appreciate it."

Daniel smiled. "Well, I enjoy hanging with you."

"So we can keep on hanging out?"

"Sure. As long as you want to."

Jerome looked up at him, his eyes brimming with tears, and he smiled, a smile that nearly broke Daniel's heart.

"Let's finish eating and head over to the lions. We're going to have to leave soon, but I want to see them."

"Okay, that's cool."

Jerome gobbled his burger and fries and was finished well before Daniel was done. He jumped up, eager to resume their visit, and sat back down immediately.

"Sorry, I thought you were done, too," he said. "I'll sit and wait."

"I can walk and eat. Let's go."

Jerome walked briskly. Daniel could tell he was trying to contain his excitement.

Daniel watched him go. The boy's happiness was infectious. He'd almost forgotten how it felt to be young. Here, Jerome had shed his *bad-boy* image. He was just an ordinary teenager, excited about life.

It was ironic how life, once so meaningless, could suddenly be so full of hope. He'd only met Renée three or four weeks ago and already his life had changed.

Despite his bravado, he'd been unconsciously scared to live again. He'd hidden it under an air of indifference… somewhat like Jerome.

Daniel dumped the half-eaten burger in a nearby garbage can. His urge to see the lions had increased.

Chapter 11

Seduction.

The word came to mind as Renée looked at her image in the mirror for the hundredth time. If she were honest with herself, she'd admit that when she'd finally decided to purchase the dress, her mind had strayed to the possibilities that wearing it entailed.

Possibilities.

That was all she'd thought about for the past few hours. The rules of the game were changing and she didn't like it one bit. Her plan had been to stay distant as she helped Daniel to deal with the tragedy in his life and start to live again.

The rules had definitely changed. She wanted to help him but she wanted him, too. After leaving the office, she found herself unable to focus, so when Cheryl had suggested she needed a new dress for the occasion, she had jumped at the chance to get him out of her mind.

It had worked for a while. Her thoughts had remained focused on shopping. Cheryl had been the perfect distraction. But he'd still been there, in the back of her mind, waiting until she was alone to continue weaving his erotic images of carnality. She sighed. The clock on the mantelpiece struck six o'clock.

Daniel had said he'd be there for six. As if on cue the doorbell rang. She grabbed her bag off the table and headed to the door.

When she opened it, she did all she could not to grab him and drag him into the house. If she were dressed to be the seducer, he definitely looked like he was ready to be seduced. He wore a black tux, which fitted him perfectly, emphasizing his rugged, serious look. He smiled, belying her stern impression of him. He looked happy, as if his day had been a good one.

"Are you ready?" he asked.

She showed him the bag in her hand, and said, "Yes, I'm ready."

She stepped outside, closing the door behind her and activated the security system. She breathed in deeply. The night had just begun. She wondered where it was all going to end.

The interior of the gallery sparkled with bright white light. They stepped out of the dark into a room that pounded with the sweet, calypso rhythm of the islands. Palm leaves were everywhere, placed artistically to give a sense of the vibrant, tropical landscape.

In one corner, a table laden with food and tropical fruit completed the picture of sultry richness.

"Daniel, over here." Taurean beckoned to them. In person, the resemblance really was uncanny.

Taking her hand, Daniel guided her toward his brother and the beautiful woman who stood at his side. Alana was even more beautiful than her photo in the newspaper.

When they reached the couple, Taurean stretched his hand out and said, "You must be Renée. It's a pleasure to meet you. I'm Taurean and this beauty next to me is my wife."

Alana stepped forward and kissed her on the cheek. "I'm delighted that you came." She turned to Daniel. "And it's great to see you, Daniel. It's been too long."

She reached out to embrace him, planting a kiss on his cheek. "You and your brother can do some more catching up. I'm going to take Renée to see my paintings."

She took Renée's hand in hers. When they were out of hearing range, she turned to Renée.

"I'm sorry to pull you away, but I just wanted to give them some time together. They haven't seen each other for so long but they'll be all right. They are both strong men, but sometimes, I don't think they realize what real strength is."

"I know what you mean. I haven't known Daniel for long, but I know he is strong. He just needs to remember it's there."

"You love him, don't you?" Alana asked. "And don't deny it. I can tell."

Renée hadn't expected the question, but now that it had been asked, the answer scared her.

"You don't have to answer. I can see it in the way you look at him. And you stepped in to reunite the brothers even though you knew Daniel didn't want you to. You don't have to answer that, either. I'm sure my suspicions are correct."

Renée was at a loss for words, but when she eventually found her voice, she said, "I can see we're going to be good friends. You can already read me like a book."

"I hope so, too. I think we have a lot in common. We both love a Buchanan man…that's reason enough to be friends. I think I'm going to like you."

Renée returned the smile. "While I'm enjoying talking about the man in my life, I really, really want to see your work. So lead the way."

"Now I really think I'm going like you."

Daniel and Taurean watched as the two most beautiful women in the room walked away.

"They're already engrossed in each other. I think we are witnessing the birth of a new friendship."

"Yeah, and we're not going to be safe when the two of them gang up on us."

"The two of them? I'm not even sure if Renée is going to be around for any length of time. I'm not sure she likes me that much."

"Don't like each other and the two of you are sleeping together?" At Daniel's expression Taurean laughed. "Yes, Bro. I can see that the two of you are making whoopee," he continued. "And I have no doubt that you'll end up in each other's arms tonight."

"Wishful thinking on my part. She's determined to keep me at arm's length."

"In that getup? That dress is made to be taken off."

"I've been taking it off all evening," Daniel said, his voice wistful. "Trust me."

"I plan to have the hot number Alana is wearing off as soon as we get back to the hotel room. Twice in one day can't hurt, right? I have to catch up on those seven years I was in prison."

Daniel paused, then said, "Look, about that time you were in prison. Well, I'm really sorry about that."

"You already told me you were," Taurean said.

"I know I did. A part of me did because I felt I had to. But I'm sorry today because I really *am* sorry. I haven't been the best brother."

"You were a little self-righteous and arrogant, yes, but you were still my brother and I love you," Taurean said. "And I never doubted you loved me. I just knew that you loved God more. And that's the way it should have been."

"I'm not even sure if that's what it was. It was more about loving me more and not letting God teach me to love," Daniel replied. "I need you to forgive me."

"Daniel, there's nothing to forgive. Just thank God we've found each other again."

"Then we're good with each other?" he tentatively asked.

"We are definitely good." Taurean smiled broadly.

"Well, now I suppose it's only fair I take you to see my wife's work. She's talented, and I'm proud of her."

He turned to lead the way and then turned back.

"Actually I want to ask you a question first and before you tell me no, I want you to think about it."

"What is it?'

"Thanksgiving is coming up. I spoke to Mom today and she's coming to Barbados. Patrick and Paula are planning to come, too. Mason still needs to confirm if he can be there. What do you say about coming to Barbados in the next two weeks? I know it's short notice, but it'd be good for the family to get together. They will want to see you. It's Thanksgiving. Even though it's not celebrated on the island, we can have our own tropical Thanksgiving."

Daniel hesitated. He wasn't sure if he was ready for a big Buchanan family gathering.

"Taurean, let me think about it for a few days. I'll let you know by the time you leave."

"Good, that's all I ask. And of course you can bring your girlfriend." At Daniel's silence, Taurean continued. "So are we are going to go through another round of denial?"

"Okay, *girlfriend.* Though it's nothing official. Like I said, she's skittish."

"So she's the skittish one?"

"And what does that mean, Bro?"

"Nothing, nothing at all. Come, let me take you to see the paintings. You have to see the big naked one of me. It always makes all the women swoon."

"You have got to be kidding!" Daniel exclaimed.

"No, I'm not. But fortunately the jewels are hidden."

"Oh, good, I was getting nervous."

Their laughter filled the gallery and all eyes turned in their direction. Daniel turned to where Alana and Renée stood. Alana frowned and put a finger to her lips, but there was a smile on her face.

Daniel's eyes captured Renée's across the room and his heart increased its pace.

He wanted her. Desired her. He trembled, his need for her so overpowering. He wasn't ready for this sense of helplessness. He was falling deeper into the swirling mist of uncertainty.

What he felt was strong, but it was too soon to be thinking of love. Inside he was still grieving for his wife and daughter.

Alana and Taurean wished them a good night and headed up to the room. Daniel turned to Renée.

"You ready to go home?" Daniel asked.

"Are you?" she responded.

He smiled. She knew exactly what he meant, but she was trying to be difficult.

"My home or yours?" he asked.

"Mine is fine," she replied. "Just a nightcap?"

"Just a nightcap," he agreed, but he smiled at her, a sly, knowing smile.

Thirty minutes later, they entered her apartment. Renée was already wondering if she'd made the right decision. They'd end up in bed and in the early hours of the morning he'd leave her alone. For some reason, she didn't want tonight to be about sex. She wanted them to spend time together, to talk, laugh and share. But to expect that would be all was wishful thinking. Men were controlled by their baser instincts.

She turned to him. "I'm going to get into something a bit more comfortable and take these heels off. You can get something to drink from the refrigerator."

"Thanks. I just want to get out of this jacket."

She turned to head to the bedroom. He was taking his jacket off and moving toward the settee. In the bedroom, she took her dress off and slipped into a large T-shirt. She smiled when she saw him. He was sprawled out on the sofa, legs up, shoes off, eyes closed.

She went back to the bedroom and returned with a blanket. She placed it over him, turned the lamp light off and headed to her bedroom. She was tired, too.

She laughed. She'd wanted them to spend some time together, talking, but he'd gone and fallen asleep. No problem. They'd talk another time. She was drained, so getting some well-deserved sleep was a blessing.

She took a quick shower and as soon as she hit the bed she was fast asleep.

During the night she woke suddenly.

"It's only me. Go back to sleep." It was Daniel.

He was lying next to her. He placed his arms around her, drawing her close to him until she was curled against him, her back against his chest.

"You feel good lying next to me. I could get used to this."

"I could, too."

He kissed the nape of her neck. "I could get used to kissing you every day, too."

She didn't answer for a moment. When she did speak, she said, "I really enjoyed tonight. Your brother is a gentleman and, Alana, I love her. After spending all day in the store shopping and then going to the hairdresser, tonight was perfect."

"Cheryl kept you busy, I see."

"Yes, she told me I had to go to the show looking like a million dollars."

"And you did."

"Thank you. You didn't look so bad yourself. Of course, I'm sure you didn't spend all day shopping and preparing."

"Definitely not. I spent it at the Brookfield Zoo."

"I've never taken you for a zoo kind of person."

"I would have you know I enjoy going to the zoo. But this time I took one of the boys from the Center. Jerome. I've been mentoring him. He's a good kid."

"He must be."

"I plan to spend some time with him. He has no parents and lives with his grandmother. He's pretty decent. Just searching for someone to care for him."

"You seem to like him a lot."

"I do. And for some reason he seems to enjoy being with me."

"He needs a father figure. And to me, you're a great choice. He chose you. Maybe God wants you to be there for him."

He didn't respond at first. "Maybe God does."

She turned to face him. “Promise me something. You won’t get attached to him and then run out on him.”

“I have no intention of doing that. I’ve retired my running shoes. I must be crazy, but I’ve actually thought of doing something permanent about it. His grandmother is concerned about him, but I don’t want to make a rash decision. I’m not even sure if I can be a good parent or guardian.”

“Well, that certainly is a big decision, but you do a fairly good job of it at the Center,” she teased. “Go talk to his grandmother and see what she says about it.”

“I just don’t want to do this and then someone special comes along in the future and doesn’t want him in our lives.”

“Then, I’d say she doesn’t deserve to have you. She’d be one selfish bitch.”

He laughed. “I didn’t know you used that kind of language.”

“Oh, I’ve been known to use a few choice words on occasion.”

“I’m impressed. How’d you like to meet Jerome?”

“Only when he’s ready. I’m not sure if he’s going to want to share you right now.”

“But he has to know that you’re going to be part of my life.”

“I don’t know. Maybe if you let him know I want to meet him he might be more accepting,” Renée suggested. “He needs to know that you will always have time for him.”

“That makes sense. But I’ll play it by ear.”

"You feeling tired?" she asked. "I can hear it in your voice."

"Yeah."

"Me, too. I just want to fall asleep in your arms."

She turned back around and snuggled into his hold. "That sounds good."

Ironically, when Daniel woke in the morning Renée was gone. He'd overslept. It was almost midday. He picked up his cell phone. Two missed calls. One from Renée. The other from Jerome.

He dialed Renée's phone but there was no response. He dialed Jerome and he answered immediately.

"You told me I could call you."

"Buddy, it's not a problem. I meant it when I said you can call me."

"Cool. Are you going to be at the Center tonight? I have basketball practice."

"I'll be there. I won't miss it."

"Good. I'll see you later. I'm going to go finish my homework."

"Okay, then."

"And do you want to go get some ice cream or something? I want to ask you about a project I have for a class."

"Yeah, ice cream would be cool."

"Okay, I'll pay. I kept some of my allowance from last week."

"Don't worry about that. I'll pay this time. I'll see you this evening. I'll be done by six."

"Cool. Later." The phone disconnected.

There was no turning back. The boy already had expectations. Not that Daniel had any intention of backing out. God had given him a second chance. It was not what he'd expected, but he'd accepted it willingly. He intended to do all he could to help Jerome to become the man he could be. He'd seen too many young boys go the way of the gun and Jerome was a prime candidate. The boy was aching for a father's love. Daniel was glad he had been there. There were so many people out there looking to exploit kids who wanted love.

Daniel remembered his father clearly and he had promised himself that he would never be the kind of father his had been. His father had never been physically abusive, it had all been about psychological control. It had only been after Taurean's release from prison, when he'd taken a good look at himself, that he had realized he had become just like his father. Now he had a chance to be the kind of person he should be. He was not Jerome's biological father, but he would teach him all he needed to know about life. The only thing he had to do now was hope Jerome liked Renée, but he knew Renée, and Daniel suspected that Jerome would soon be as hooked on her as he was.

Since he was making calls, he picked the phone up and called Taurean. One more day and his brother would be leaving. He planned on going over to the hotel tonight after he dropped Jerome home. Taurean answered immediately.

"Daniel, thanks for coming last night. Alana and I really appreciated it."

"I enjoyed myself. Alana is really talented. You must

be proud of her. I noticed that Renée liked one of the paintings so I bought it, but I don't plan to let her know until Christmas."

"I'll make sure Alana puts a discount price on it."

"No need to do that. Remember, I'm still a rich man. I haven't touched much of the money I got when Dad died or the insurance money from the accident."

"That's good, but I'm still going to pay for your ticket and Renée's ticket to Barbados. I did invite you, after all, and I'm not taking no for an answer."

"No problem. But I still have to talk with my boss. So what's the plan for the day?"

"Alana and I are just going over to the gallery. I'm hoping you have some time to drop by but we leave tomorrow. I'm sorry we didn't come for more than the four days, but neither of us likes leaving the kids for too long. Plus, I never would've thought I'd run into you."

"I always knew you'd be a good father."

"And you, too. You were a good father. You were gentler. Chelsea transformed you."

"Maybe, my brother. I may soon find out what it's like again."

"Renée is pregnant?"

"No, Taurean. There is a boy at the Center whom I've been hanging with, mentoring. I'm actually thinking of letting him move in with me. Her grandmother is worried about him and she's not doing too well, healthwise. I plan on asking her to let him come live with me. He has no one else. I could eventually make it permanent. But taking on the responsibility of a teenager is vastly different from an infant."

"Well, I say go for it. I'm sure you'll be good for him."

"Thanks for the vote of confidence."

"No problem, man. So we'll see you later, right? I have to go, though…Alana is calling. Breakfast in bed."

"Okay, Bro. You go enjoy your breakfast and don't hurt yourself. Tell Alana have mercy on the old man."

"Old man? For me, breakfast has a number of courses and I'm more than capable of partaking of each. I'll see you later."

Daniel put the phone down. The conversation floated around in his head. Taurean had actually thought Renée was pregnant. He would love to see Renée pregnant with his child. She would be even more beautiful, blooming with their son or daughter.

Last night had been different. They'd hardly touched, but he felt a sense of belonging he'd not felt for ages. She'd felt it, too. Of that he was certain. He loved her, but was that enough to dream about a lifetime of commitment? On the other hand, marrying her would be perfect if he were to adopt Jerome or become his guardian. Renée would make a wonderful mother. The maternal instinct came naturally to her. He'd seen how she had dealt with Jamie. She'd been gentle and understanding.

But he needed to pause a bit. He was getting ahead of himself with his plans. Suppose Jerome's grandmother didn't agree. But he knew he wanted to be the boy's father in every sense of the word, and God would make it work if it was part of his plan.

He stopped suddenly. He'd not asked God anything in the past two or three years. Something heavy and cold unwrapped itself from around his heart. He felt lighter, free. Like the prodigal son, he was acknowledging that he'd been wrong. God was taking care of him, despite the way he'd turned away from Him. He was ready to live again.

Tonight when he called Taurean, he'd let him know when he was going to the island. Maybe Barbados would be his final place of healing.

It had given healing to both Alana and Taurean, and maybe, just maybe, he'd find rest from his weariness there.

Chapter 12

Daniel looked at the most distressingly large pile of ice cream he'd ever seen and his mouth watered. He settled for a simple banana split, but what Jerome was eating with gusto left him wishing he'd made the same choice.

"Man, this is so good, I may get another one," Jerome said, the expression on his face one of utter delight.

"While I find it rather tempting, I'm not going to allow you to eat another one. That must be so bad for your health you'll put on twenty pounds before we even leave here."

Jerome laughed. "Not going to happen," he said. "My metabolism will take care of the excess. If you were my dad, your grocery bill would be so high." Jerome stopped immediately. He looked embarrassed.

Daniel realized this was the opportunity he'd wanted. "That may not be such a bad thing."

"What do you mean?" Jerome said.

"Would you have a problem with me being your dad?"

The boy hesitated. "You mean like a foster dad?"

"No, not a foster parent. I mean like a real dad. Make it legal."

"I'll get to call you dad?"

"Only if you want to."

"I mean, only if you wouldn't mind."

"That's the way I'd want it. But you have to promise me something. That you'd always try to be the best person you can be."

"That shouldn't be too hard. I have a good example to follow." He said this slowly.

Daniel could see he wanted to cry. Man, he was torn up inside, too.

"You wanna leave here? I should talk to your grandmother in person. This can't happen until I've spoken to her and she agrees."

"I'm sure she'll agree. She's worried about me. She'll agree to anything that will keep me off the streets. Not that I planned to ever go here. I don't want to be like those other kids out there. Don't be fooled by how I dress. I'm nothing like those guys. It's just survival."

"I know, son. I know."

The smile on Jerome's face was enough to make everything right.

But…there was still his relationship with Renée to worry about.

* * *

Daniel knocked on the door of Shelley's apartment. He wasn't sure if she was at home, but he wanted to talk to her. She was the one person who could help him deal with his confused state of mind.

An eye appeared at the peephole and then the clanking of the several locks on her door. The door opened and she stood there, white stuff plastered on her face and wrapped in a robe that had seen better days.

He tried not to laugh out loud, but it took all of his self-control not to.

"If you dare laugh, I'm going to fire you," she said, glaring at him.

He did laugh this time. "You know you need me in the office. Who's going to cover your back if you get rid of me?"

"All right, I hear you. Come on in. Who am I to argue with the best assistant I've ever had?" She turned around and headed for the living room, leaving him to lock the door.

When he was done, he followed her, joining her on the sofa where she spent more of her time at home. Shelley loved game shows, and as he expected, an ancient episode of the *$25,000 Pyramid* with Dick Clark was on her television.

"So what's wrong with my friend?" she asked. "Falling in love has you all confused and uncertain?"

He wondered how she always knew what was wrong with him. Maybe that's the reason he was here. He knew Shelley's intuition kicked in about personal matters related to him.

"It's Renée and my family," he replied. "Things are moving a bit too fast for me. When I came to Chicago, I came knowing that I needed to heal; that my time of grieving had to come to an end." He drew in a deep breath before he continued. "I wanted change and I was slowly coming to accept that. Now I'm faced with a budding relationship and my family wants me back in their lives. It's overwhelming."

"Are you here for me to give you validation for what you already know you want to do?"

"Maybe." Daniel shrugged. "I'm not sure. Renée makes me feel alive. I've been emotionally dead for so long, I don't know if I should get involved with the first woman who catches my interest and makes me feel good."

Shelley moved closer to him, placing a hand on his arm. Her touch offered comfort, which radiated through his body, soothing him with its warmth.

"You love her, Daniel. And the sooner you are willing to admit it, the sooner you'll be able to deal with what's happening with you."

"Love?" Daniel replied. "I'm not even sure I want to love again. I've loved people and it has brought pain and loss."

"But those are the realities of life," Shelley said, almost apologetically. "We live and we die. Everyone you know and love will one day die. Some before you, others long after you are gone. That doesn't mean you love them any less. I would think it would mean you love them even more. You were a minister. You of all people should know that. You keep denying God and saying that the two of you have come to some understanding, but that's just an excuse."

He nodded in agreement. "You're right. Maybe going to Barbados will help me deal with this. I have to face my family."

"You know what your real problem is, Daniel?" she asked. "You're a man. You want to be strong and courageous. And yes, that's part of what being a man is. But you needed to dig deeper and find the true man inside, the man who, despite his strength, knows how to cry. Have you cried for the woman and child you claim to love so much? When that happens, then you'll truly start to heal."

He didn't respond, didn't know what to say. In fact there was no need for words. Shelley had said it all. Her hand squeezed his. He squeezed hers back gently, then released it and stood. She glanced up at him, her eyes searching his face, as if she would find the answers there.

"Thank you," he said, pressing his palm against her cheek.

"No thanks necessary," she replied. "That's what friends are for. Now leave me alone so I can watch this show. All you need to do is look into your heart and the answers will all be there." She smiled broadly.

"I love you," he said.

She didn't respond, only continued to watch her show now on the screen, but he knew she'd heard. He turned and walked away, his heart feeling lighter.

He needed to get home and make a call. He planned on asking Renée to go with him to Barbados.

* * *

Renée closed the door behind her and tossed her briefcase on the sofa. She'd actually left work at the end of her shift. Today had been a particularly good one. Nothing major had happened and she'd made a serious dent in her paperwork. She'd even gone out to lunch with Cheryl—a rare occurrence.

She moved to the bedroom and slipped out of her clothes, then headed to the shower. Tonight she had all intentions of pampering herself. Life was too good to be worried about the little things.

She filled the tub, making sure that the water was warm and poured in her favorite scented bubble bath. When she stepped into the tub and lowered herself into the water, she felt like a baby cocooned in its mother's womb. She closed her eyes, and as her body slowly relaxed, the fatigue drained from her. In the midst of her daydreaming, she heard a noise in the distance.

Her doorbell. Who on earth could that be?

She pulled herself up, dried herself quickly and slipped on a robe. She rushed from the bathroom, moved quickly to the door, unlocked it and swung it open.

Daniel.

A part of her had known it was him, but she tried not to acknowledge it. Now her heart pounded in her chest with the excitement of seeing him.

She stepped back instinctively, giving him confirmation that he could enter.

As he stepped inside he reached for her, drawing her toward him until her breasts pressed against his chest.

"Don't you know you should check to see who's at the door before you open it?" he scolded.

"I'm sorry. I wasn't thinking."

"This may be a good neighborhood but you still need to be careful."

She didn't respond. She kept staring at his lips.

"You were in the shower?"

"I was taking a bath."

"Now, if I'd known that I would have come earlier," he teased.

He drew her closer and she pressed herself against him.

"If I'd known you were coming I would have waited."

"I should have called," he apologized.

"We'll have time for a shower a bit later," she said seductively. "Right now, I want you. I've been thinking of making love to you all day."

He lowered his head to capture her lips in a kiss that screamed desire. Renée placed her hands around his neck, pulling him even closer. She felt her body quiver with excitement, with the commanding intrusion of his tongue. She reached for his zipper, wanting to feel him deep inside her.

"Come, let's go to the bedroom," he said, between the caress of their lips.

"No, I want you here, right here!"

"Oh, so you want to be kinky. I can do kinky." He laughed.

Her hands continued their task, allowing his pants to fall to the ground. His boxers followed and he felt her hands on his penis, her fingers running gently along its length. He groaned softly, knowing that he could not wait. He quickly removed his shirt and watched as her robe fell to the ground, revealing her perfect nude body.

"So you were waiting for me?" he moaned, carrying her toward the table.

He set her down, moved between her legs and then lowered her back to the table. He moved his head downward, placing his mouth on her stomach and then trailing down until he was between her legs.

He parted her lips with a finger, his mouth finding access to the core of her womanhood. Beneath him, her body shuddered and twisted while small whimpers of pleasure flowed from her lips. He buried his tongue deep inside her, the fresh scent of the lavender heightening his enjoyment. He teased her sensitive nub, arousing her to the point of exhilaration before he brought her down again, only to take her back up until she screamed with her need. He tasted the sweet honey of her femininity. And then, her body stiffened and her face came alive with the delight of her orgasm.

Her legs parted and he stood up and poised his hardness at her entrance, probing, teasing, rubbing until she'd bit down on her lips, trying to hold her cries inside. He slipped inside her slowly, loving the feel of her tight walls against his erect length. He pushed deep and her muscles clenched around him, drawing every thick, long inch within her. His penis throbbed and he began a firm thrusting of his hips back and forward.

He maintained a steady rhythm, his eyes focused on

her, watching as her face gave away the pleasure she felt. He stopped temporarily, shifting her until her buttocks touched the edge of the table. She wrapped her legs round his waist, drawing him closer and deeper.

"Don't stop, Daniel," she commanded. "It feels so good."

"You love it, don't you? Tell me you love it."

"Yes," she replied, her mouth covering one of his nipples.

He loved the feel of her mouth on him. His arousal intensified and he increased his pace, stroking her strong and firm. She groaned and called his name, urging him on, praising his prowess until his only desire was to please her and give her the same joy he was experiencing. When the moment of release came, it surprised them both with its power.

Daniel cried out in pleasure, his body tensing and relaxing as wave after wave of heat coursed through him, the feeling so powerful that he wished it would never stop. Renée held on to him, her own orgasm as forceful as his. Her fingernails pressed into his back but he felt no pain, only the vulnerability of her body as it shook uncontrollably against his.

He lifted her and carried her with him into the bathroom. They both needed the soothing silkiness of warm water against their bodies to stem the heat. But Daniel had no doubt they'd make love again.

Tonight was going to be a long night of ultimate pleasure and he had all intentions of playing his part.

* * *

Daniel nibbled on Renée's neck again. She giggled, tapping him gently on the stomach.

"So what do you say? Are you willing to go with me to Barbados?" he asked again, his hand gently kneading a taut nipple.

She hesitated. The offer had come as a surprise, but it was a tempting one. She was due a vacation since she hadn't taken one since she started work at the hospital. Leaving for a week or two couldn't hurt. She was sure getting the time off should not be a problem. But she couldn't concentrate on what he was asking. She slapped his hand away playfully.

"Are you sure it won't be a problem with your family?" she asked.

"Definitely not. Taurean was the one who suggested I invite you. You only have to agree. Just image all that sunshine, the white sand and crystal-clear water."

She laughed. "Okay, you are really tempting me now…and I do want to see the island."

"Plus I'm doing what you suggested. I want to see my family, and what better time than at Thanksgiving? And I want you with me."

"You're sure you're ready to face them?" she asked.

"Yes, I know I'm ready. Seems that I just needed the push. Seeing Taurean made a difference. I know that I left Brooklyn and my family, but I wonder if I hadn't left if I would have dealt with my situation better."

"Maybe, or maybe not. But you did take a long hard

look at the man you were. Maybe you needed to be away from your family and friends to do that."

He nodded thoughtfully. "That's true."

"So where do I come into all this?" she asked.

"I want to be honest with you. I care about you. I enjoy being with you, but I'm not sure I'm ready for anything more."

"I feel the same way. Since I got jilted at the altar, I've been wary of relationships. I'm not sure if this is the best thing for me, but I'm willing to give it a try."

"I can only imagine how that affected you. I can only promise you that I won't ever intentionally hurt you. I'm not one for making love without commitment. I may not be the minister I was before, but I'm still not happy with just having sex for having sex. I care about you."

"Then we're in agreement. I don't want to be a booty call. That's not the kind of person I am, but as you said, I'm uncertain, too. Maybe I'll go to Barbados with you. That way we can use the time there to see if this is more than just a romp between the sheets."

"Well, how about we romp between the sheets right now? I want to make love to you again."

Her hands gripped his hardness tightly and it jerked in her hands. Damn, he was definitely ready for her again. He rolled her over onto her back, poised himself above her and shifted her legs apart with his knees. He looked down at her, seeing the sweltering heat in her eyes. He captured her lips in a passionate kiss and set out to show her how much making love to her gave him pleasure.

* * *

Daniel walked into the Center feeling as if he were walking on air. It was a bit of a cliché but in his case it was completely true. His feet felt light and his body felt agile.

He left Renée's apartment in the early hours of the morning, reluctantly. He'd watched her as she slept and knew that if he were honest with himself he would admit that what he felt for her went further that just attraction. Even now he didn't want to say the word. But in time he knew he'd have to face up to the reality of what was happening to him.

Shelley stepped out of her office as he was about to knock on her door.

"Morning, Shelley," he practically chirped.

"You're very cheerful this morning, Mr. Buchanan. I'm wondering what, or should I say who, is responsible for that aura of satisfaction." She bent her head closer to his, her brown eyes sparkling, and whispered, "Can I assume that it is the lovely Ms. Walker?"

He laughed, but the look on his face told it all.

Shelley squealed and placed her hands over her eyes. "Oh, my, the image in my mind is too vivid. This is not good for an aging individual like me who doesn't get any."

They laughed.

"On a more serious note," he said, "and so that our colleagues don't think that we've gone crazy, I need to take some vacation time in the next few weeks. Over Thanksgiving. I've decided that I'm going to Barbados."

"That's good. The best idea I've heard in months."

"Renée will be going with me."

She squealed again. "Oh, a tropical wedding!"

"Shelley," Daniel cautioned, "we're going to Barbados for a family reunion that my brother Taurean has planned. That's it. Nothing more," he emphasized.

"So you say. You mark my word, there's going to be a tropical wedding some day soon."

"I hear you," he responded. "And now I think you better go on your way," he said with a smirk. "Just want to know if I can have the time."

"Of course you can. Haven't I been trying to encourage you to take some time off? You haven't taken a vacation in the two years you've been here," she commented. "What about Jerome?" she added.

"I'll talk to him today when he comes in. I wish I could take him with me, but he has exams coming up. I'm meeting with his grandmother this evening about letting him come to stay with me. I've mentioned it to her on the phone. She's worried about him. She's sick and there is no one to take care of him. She and I don't want him to end up in the system."

"I'm sorry to hear about her. But are you sure you want to do this?" she asked.

"I'm sure. I know I want to take care of him. I know I'm ready to be a father again. Maybe this is part of my healing."

"Good, I'm hoping it all works itself out. He's a good boy and just needs someone like you in his life. Plus he'll be gaining two in one."

"Two in one?"

"Yes, a dad and a mom," she replied, chuckling.

"You're too much. Just don't count my chickens before they hatch."

"Oh, I never do, but I'm going to tell Jerome he's going to have to call me Aunty Shelley." She paused. "That sounds so good."

He glared at her.

"Okay, I'll leave you. I'm going over to meet with the mayor. He wants us to work on an upcoming program. Sounds interesting and should bring us some great funding." She walked away, whistling loudly.

It was only as he turned to walk to his office that he realized she was whispering, "I'm Getting Married in the Morning."

Of course, Cheryl's reaction to her upcoming trip made Renée wonder if she was doing to right thing.

"Oh, you're going to have some great sex under the tropical moonlight. I wish I could come with you," Cheryl whined.

"But you'd have to bring Julian along. I'm sure he wouldn't want you finding some hunky island boy."

"Me? Leave Julian? Definitely not! I was only allowing my oversexed mind to dream. I just read the most fabulous romance set on the islands. It was so hot I had to turn up the air-conditioning. Poor Julian didn't sleep at all that night." She giggled. "Not that he complained. He has more energy that I do. Sometimes I have to tell him I have a headache just to take a break. And then in the middle of the night, I forget all about the headache and we're doing it like rabbits."

"Both of you need help," Renée teased. "I'm surprised that either of you can walk with all the sex you're having."

"And on that note, I'm going to have to say goodbye. I hear Julian calling me from the bathroom. It's George Benson night..."

"George Benson night? As I said, both of you are sick. Have fun."

"Definitely." The phone disconnected, but not before she heard Cheryl yell, "I'm coming, honeypoo!"

Renée placed the phone down, unable to control her laughter. Cheryl and Julian were the perfect couple and she wondered why after a year of dating they hadn't made the final step. She'd never seen two people who were more in love. Well, except in the picture on the mantelpiece at her parent's home. The picture was one of the few memories of her father, but each time she looked at it, the love she saw in her father's eyes was the kind of love she wanted for herself. Her mother's words over the years had only served to confirm that her parents had been madly in love. Maybe that's why her mother never ceased her matchmaking. She only wanted what she'd had for her daughter.

Tonight she'd pay her mother a visit. In the past few weeks she hadn't even been over for dinner or lunch. Strange enough, her mother hadn't called about any new dates she'd set up. She definitely had to go visit. She wanted to tell her mother about Daniel.

Tomorrow she'd talk to her supervisor and let him know of her plans. She wanted things to work out with Daniel. She'd thought long and hard after their night of passion and she knew she loved him. Her admission had not been earth-shattering, like in the romance novels she read, but it had come with a simple acceptance of what she'd long known but had refused to acknowledge.

She loved him. Loved everything about the troubled, stubborn man who hadn't even tried to charm her. He was a special individual and didn't even know it. His devotion to the Center, his willingness to take time out to see Jamie and his commitment to a young boy who needed a father. All these things made him the wonderful individual he was.

She could almost hear her mother now. *It's about time. Let's go shopping. I know where to find the perfect wedding dress.*

But for now, these were her fantasies. She knew Daniel liked her, cared for her, and though Cheryl claimed that she was sure he loved her, to expect more would be to be two steps ahead of where their relationship was.

Even if he loved her, there was nothing that said he would marry her. She knew that, even now, memories of his past still haunted him. But that didn't mean she would give up. If ever there was a chance for her to find her happily ever after, now was the time.

So she'd go with him to the island. She'd be herself. And hopefully, the island would work its magic and under the midnight moon they'd share magical kisses and declare their love for each other.

She walked out onto the balcony and inhaled deeply. In the distant sky, a star hurled its way across the darkness. She smiled. Memories of another time she'd stood here came back to her vivid and clear, almost as if she'd stepped back in time.

"Maybe...just maybe," she whispered into the night. "I have found true love."

Chapter 13

Daniel stepped into the elevator and pressed for the fifth floor, amazed when the contraption actually moved upward. He felt a bit uncomfortable. This was the first time he would be visiting Jerome's home. Usually, when they spent time together, Jerome would meet him at the Center. He'd spoken on several occasions to the teenager's grandmother, but never met her in person.

The elevator stopped with a groan and he thanked God that he'd reached his destination safely. He walked down the dirty hallway until he reached apartment 509. He knocked on the door. It opened immediately, and Jerome stood there smiling broadly.

"Yo, man."

They did their usual knock and Jerome stepped back so he could enter.

The apartment was tiny and clean, but it took him a while to adjust to the dimly lit interior. An elderly woman sat there, her eyes focused on him.

She smiled as he approached her. She was frail and seemed tired, but there was a twinkle in her eyes.

"So you're the Mr. Buchanan who my grandson's always talking about. Come sit here so we can talk. Jerome, you go to your room while we adults chat." Her voice was surprisingly strong.

When Jerome made his exit, she turned to him. "So you want to take care of my grandson?"

"Yes, ma'am," he said. He felt like a little boy being interrogated by a principal.

"You think I can't take care of my grandson?"

"Not at all, ma'am," he replied.

"Well I can't," she said emphatically. "I'm dying. It's cancer. And there is no one to take care of him when I'm gone. The only person is his good-for-nothing uncle. I don't want that man anywhere around Jerome when I'm gone. He's bad and I thank God each day for letting my grandson go to that Center. He's been a different boy. I've seen the change in him. I've seen how you helped to change him." She paused, coughing loudly, her body wracked with spasms.

He stood, moving to assist her, but with a flick of her hand, she ushered him back to his seat.

"It's all right. There's not much you can do. I can take care of myself. I didn't live for eighty-two years for nothing. But thanks for the help. You're a good man."

"Thank you," Daniel replied.

"Well, I don't see that I have much of a choice. I don't

have anywhere else for him to go, but besides that, I can see you're a good man. Get me a lawyer and we can take care of the legalities. At least when I die, I know he's in good hands. You have a girlfriend?"

"Yes," he answered immediately.

"Good, Jerome needs a father, but he needs a mother, too. A woman's touch is good. You plan on marrying her?"

"If she'll have me."

She laughed. "Oh, so she's giving you a bit of trouble? That's good. A man needs to do a bit of chasing so he appreciates what he wants. I remember giving my late husband a long chase. Made him wait until our wedding night." She laughed loudly, but broke into another fit of coughing.

When she finally stopped, she said. "You can call the boy now. Where are you taking him?"

"My girlfriend and I are taking him to the movies. She hasn't met him yet."

She smiled. "That's good."

He stood and headed toward where Jerome had disappeared.

"One more thing," she said. He stopped and turned.

"You take care of my grandson good. I want him to grow up to be a good, God-fearing man. I know I won't get to see that but that's my wish."

"I promise. You have nothing to be worried about."

"Then I can die in peace. You make sure you bring that girlfriend here and let me see her. If she's going to be my grandson's mother, I got to see her."

"I'll do that as soon as possible."

Daniel walked down the corridor and knocked on the door of room Jerome had entered.

The boy came out, concern on his face.

"You ready to go?" Daniel asked.

"Yes, sure. I've been ready. I can't wait to see this movie."

"You sure you up to having my girl along."

"It's cool, man. As long as she's not one of those snobs. She better be cool."

"I promise you, she *is* cool."

"Good, let's go."

Daniel followed him back to the sitting room. Jerome bent down to hug and kiss his grandmother.

"Have a good time. Mr. Buchanan, you come here and give me a hug, too," she said.

Daniel complied. The old lady was something else.

"Is she going to get here soon?" Jerome asked for the hundredth time.

"Jerome, didn't I tell you she'd be here in the next five minutes or so. We got here early."

"I know, I know. I'm just looking forward to meeting her. Just want to see what kind of girl my main man likes."

"Okay, well, your wait is over. She's coming."

Jerome immediately turned in the direction Daniel was looking. His mouth stayed wide open, but he composed himself quickly.

"Man, you've got good taste. She's one hot…" He stopped. "Sorry, I didn't mean any disrespect."

"It's fine. I *know* she's hot." They both laughed.

Daniel greeted her with a kiss on the cheek when she reached them.

Renée turned to Jerome, smiling. "And who's this handsome young man?"

Before Daniel could respond, Jerome stuck a hand out. "Jerome," he replied. "Nice to meet you."

"A gentleman, too," Renée said. "It's great to meet you, too." With that, she placed her arms around him and hugged him.

"You gentlemen ready to go watch this movie?" she asked, putting her arm on Jerome's shoulder, who looked up at her with devoted eyes.

"Yes, I'm ready," Jerome replied.

She turned to Daniel. "Who's paying?" she teased.

Daniel smiled, his heart soaring with love for her. Everything was going to be all right. He took her hand and together they all walked into the theater.

Chapter 14

The island of Barbados stretched below the aircraft as it dipped gently before making its final descent. Hundreds of lights twinkled below.

Daniel couldn't wait to explore the island. He'd only been here a short time when Taurean got married, but this time was different. As soon as the reunion dinner and the other planned activities were over, he would go exploring. He wanted to savor the island's rich culture and beauty. He hoped Renée would join him.

Next to him, Renée stirred in her sleep. They had chatted briefly before she had eventually closed her eyes and fallen asleep. He'd been unable to sleep, despite the tiredness that overpowered him. Thoughts of his family had taken him through a range of emotions. He was slowly coming to grips with the changes in his life—his family, Renée and Jerome. Each one of them was important to him and he was coming closer to an understanding of how each of them would fit into his life and future.

Since Jerome's "date" with Renée, they had connected well, right off the bat. Renée had discovered that he had a voracious appetite for reading and had presented him with the full series of Harry Potter books. Daniel had spent several hours listening to them discuss the books and watching the movies. Not his usual fare, but he'd been happy that they had bonded.

Of course, Jerome had been unhappy that he couldn't go with them to Barbados for the two weeks, but Daniel had promised him that they would spend the next summer on the island. He'd been adamant that Jerome not miss school. He also promised Jerome that he and Renée would call each day.

He smiled. He'd grown to love the boy like his own flesh and blood. He couldn't imagine his life without him. Jerome had even started calling him Dad teasingly, but he knew that for the boy it was something he wanted. The first time he'd not been sure how to react. Instead, Daniel had almost crushed him with a tight bear hug.

As the plane descended, he gently shook Renée awake. Soon the aircraft was taxiing to Gate 12.

Thirty minutes later, and after enduring the long lines at Immigration and Customs, Daniel and Renée stepped into the warm Bajan night.

"Daniel! Renée! Over here!"

They turned in the direction of the voice and there, waving like crazy, was Alana.

"Come, Taurean is in the parking lot," Alana said, hugging them when they reached her. "I'll call him so he can come pick us up here."

She took her cell from her bag and punched in the number. Five minutes later, Taurean's blue SUV pulled up. The luggage was quickly loaded and they were soon on their way.

"So how was the flight?" Taurean asked, as the car pulled out onto the highway.

"Smooth, but long," Daniel replied. "Renée slept three of the four hours from Miami. I tried to sleep but couldn't, so I finally watched the movie. Of course, I'd seen it three times already, so that didn't help much."

There was laughter from the backseat. Renée and Alana were continuing their bonding.

"It's almost ten o'clock here, but Alana kept dinner warming for you. I know you must be hungry since you left Chicago early this morning. Two flights in one day can be exhausting," Taurean said.

"I know I'll be sleeping as soon as my head hits the pillow. Is Mom still arriving tomorrow?" Daniel asked.

"Yes, she's coming with Patrick and Paula," Taurean replied. "She doesn't like to travel on her own. I'm trying to see if I can get her to stay on the island for a while, especially for the winter months."

"I can see you have no intention of going back to the U.S.," Daniel observed.

"No, Alana and I love it here on the island. The kids have their friends and are happy at school. The resort is doing well and Alana gets her inspiration here. We try to visit the U.S. at least once every year. We did promise the kids we would take them to Disney World next summer. Joanne is only four and she keeps talking about meeting her favorite characters."

"You must let me know when you're going. I'd like to take Jerome and Renée."

"That's a plan. I'll let you know when we finalize the dates," Taurean said.

"We're still here, gentlemen, feeling ignored. I know how excited you are to see each other, but..." Alana complained from the back.

"My apologies, honey," Taurean said, laughter evident in his voice. "But we thought you ladies wanted to catch up. It's all but four weeks since you met and you've been chatting on the phone at least once a week," he replied as the car pulled into a driveway. "I'm sure you have lots of opportunities to talk to Daniel."

"Of course Renée and I have been catching up," Alana said. "She's my new BFF."

"BFF?" Taurean asked. "What's that?"

"You don't listen to your daughter. It means best friend forever."

They all laughed as the car came to a stop before a magnificent two-story house. Even in the shadows of night, the house stood majestically.

"Welcome to our home," Alana said as they stepped out of the car. "You'll be able to see it better in the morning, but it's our pride and joy. It was finished only a few months ago. The resort is about half a mile in that direction. You'll get a chance to see it tomorrow sometime. Come on, let's go in."

While Daniel and Taurean unloaded the luggage, the ladies went inside. When Daniel entered the house five minutes later, he stopped in his tracks. The interior of the house was just as beautiful as the outside. Shades of white and green gave the appearance of space and freshness. Paintings on the wall provided splashes of color, but did not detract from the mood the designer had tried to achieve; beautiful landscapes, subtle abstracts and a few portraits of the members of the family.

"Your portrait is the only one missing," Alana said, pointing at an empty space next to Mason's. "Hopefully you'll let me work on yours so it can be added. It's been missing for too long."

"I'll make the time," he replied, his heart feeling lighter. He knew he was home.

Daniel watched as his brother stood and stretched. They'd spent the last hour with each other. Daniel could tell by his brother's posture that he was tired.

Alana and Renée had disappeared after they'd eaten and he and his brother had remained on the balcony of Daniel's room talking.

"I have to go, my brother. I'm going to fall asleep here if I don't retire soon. Alana told me earlier that she planned on finishing a painting tonight, so I shouldn't expect her for a few hours."

"It's fine. We have time to catch up. I don't leave for two weeks."

"Well good then. I'll see you in the morning. Renée's room is just next door," he said for the tenth time, a sly smile on his face.

Daniel took the pillow off the bed and in one smooth movement threw it at his brother, who ducked, laughing loudly.

"Missed, but I see you haven't lost your skill."

"I've been chasing you out of my room for years. So yeah, I've had a lot of practice."

Before he knew what was happening, Taurean had crossed the room and wrapped his arms around him.

"Damn, Bro, it's so good to see you. You know I love you, man."

Daniel didn't respond immediately. He just wanted to enjoy the love his brother so freely offered. Taurean had always been the caring one; even though Daniel had treated him as if he were the biggest sinner on earth.

It felt strange after all these years. His brothers had always been close but he'd always been the distant one. He'd scoffed at the hugging and affection. Now he yearned for it. This bonding with his brother made him feel important, special and cared for.

He noticed the pain in Taurean's eyes.

"I'm sorry," Daniel said. "I'm glad we can have a new start. Forget the past."

Taurean smiled and nodded. "I know. I understand."

With that Taurean turned, exited the room and closed the door behind him.

Daniel wanted to call him back to try to explain further, but it didn't make any sense. He was scared. Caring about people scared him and he didn't know what to do about it. But he planned to work on it.

Renée had said that much, and maybe his time here in Barbados would help. She'd forced him to face himself, to face the unfeeling man he'd once been. But who was he now? He wasn't even sure. A work in progress? Maybe.

He didn't much like who he'd been, but he knew the person he was becoming was better, more in touch with his feelings.

There was a knock on the door.

"Come in," he responded, expecting Renée.

The door opened and his sister-in-law stood there.

"I just wanted to tell you how glad we are to have you here. We missed you."

He scoffed at what she said, but when he looked at her he saw her sincerity and chided himself.

"Thanks. It's really good to be here."

"You'll get to see the children in the morning. Taurean takes them to the beach every Saturday. I think they believe they are water nymphs."

"I can't wait to see them." He didn't realize just how much until he said it.

"I'll see you in the morning. We usually eat breakfast when the kids and Taurean return from the beach, so if you don't go with them, you'll definitely see them when they return."

"I'm an early riser. I'll be down early. And thanks for everything," Daniel replied.

"It's no problem, Daniel. You're family. See you in the morning." With a final smile, she closed the door quietly behind her.

The emptiness of the room made him realize how alone he was. He slipped out of his clothes and headed for the shower.

Tomorrow, he would have to face his mother and brothers. Another chapter in the saga that was his life.

There was a knock on his door. Taurean again? Didn't his brother know he wanted to get some sleep? Jet lag was slowly creeping into his bones.

"Come in," he said.

Renée walked in.

To say he was surprised was an understatement. He ached for her, but somehow he'd expected she would stay away.

"And how can I help you, Ms.?" he asked.

"I hope you don't mind if I sleep in here. I don't want to sleep on my own. No expectations. I just want to be with you."

"That's fine. This bed is large enough for the both of us." He shifted over, giving her the left side.

Renée joined him and slipped between the covers. She leaned over and kissed him on the lips.

"Good night," she said, before she placed her head on the pillow, drew closer to him and fell asleep.

Long after, Daniel still lay awake. His body was tired and he needed to focus on sleeping, but having Renée in his arms heightened his awareness. Again he realized how much he loved having her in his arms. He didn't know where they were going from here, but he knew he wanted her in his life permanently.

He'd use the two weeks here to convince her that being with him wouldn't be so bad, that they could have a good life together. Of course, he'd complicated matters with Jerome, but she had said that having Jerome around was no problem, and they had bonded easily.

All he had to do now was hope his family liked and approved of her. Not that it totally mattered. He would never let that determine his future.

She'd already proven herself with Alana, and Taurean had already given his blessing. He knew the others would love her. There wasn't anything about her not to love. Renée possessed beauty inside and out, and for that alone, he loved her.

Morning came in a blaze of glory. Daniel stood on the balcony looking out at the ocean in the distance. God's grandeur had never been more evident than in the colors of the tropical sunrise.

In that moment, he realized something; that he was finally ready to make peace with God. He'd been stubborn, had always been, but during his months of trying to find a peace of mind, he had failed to acknowledge a simple reality, that God was still very much a part of his life, and despite his anger and his rejection of God, He still loved Daniel.

He'd been up for hours, unable to sleep. He inhaled the clean morning air. He could live here, but his work in Chicago was not done. There was healing in the whisper of the gentle breeze wafting against his skin and in the quiet tranquility. Daniel closed his eyes and lowered himself to his knees, reverence in his heart. Humbled, he talked to God in a way he had never done before. In the past, it had been all about him and what he wanted. Tears fell from his eyes; tears for his wife and child; and tears for the fact he'd finally come to an understanding of the unending limits of God's love.

He turned around, his eyes resting on the woman who lay in his bed. God had brought her into his life. She'd helped him to live again.

Below him, he heard voices and laughter. He looked down and saw his brother and two girls. Must be Melissa and Joanne. "Taurean," he shouted.

His brother looked up. "I thought you'd still be sleeping. Want to go to the beach? You'll get to see your two nieces."

"I'll be right down," he replied.

He grabbed a shirt and rummaged around in his suitcase until he found the swim trunks he'd brought. He glanced at Renée. She was still sleeping. Oh, well, there would be time for her to get to the sea.

He dressed quickly and left the room, rushing down the stairs. He passed Alana on the way out, kissed her briefly on the cheek and raced out the back door in record time. He came to a quick stop.

"Morning, Uncle Daniel," Melissa said. She'd grown so much and already possessed her mother's beauty.

"Morn, Uncle Dan," Joanne said. "You look just like my daddy."

"Hi, Melissa. Hi, Joanne. Yes, I look like your daddy—just much better-looking," he teased.

"You're funny, Uncle Dan," Joanne said, and she reached for his hand. "You're coming to the sea with us? I can teach you how to swim."

"Thanks, honey. It's fine. I can swim, so we can spend all our time having fun."

"That's good. Come on. Let's go, Daddy. We're already late," Melissa said.

Joanne led the way, holding Daniel's hand as they walked along the rocky pathway. Soon the vast Atlantic Ocean stretched out before them.

"Come on, let's dive in," shouted Melissa, already running toward the sea.

Reaching the water's edge, she poised and dived into the oncoming water with the skill of years of practice. Taurean followed with equal skill.

"You ready to go in, Uncle Daniel?"

"Yes, sweetheart, but I'll be holding your hand as we walk or jump in. No pretty diving for me."

Joanne giggled. "Me, either, but I can swim good."

"Good," he replied, laughing at how her chest puffed up with pride. "I can swim good, too."

He helped her down to the water and helped her to "jump" in.

For an hour, they frolicked in the water, their laughter floating on the warm, tropical breeze until Joanne and Melissa drifted out to lie on the large beach towels on the sand. Soon the girls were fast asleep under an umbrella.

Lying next to each other, the brothers absorbed the rhythm of the day—the steady splash of waves against the shore, the swaying of the tall palm trees in the wind and the occasional hawk of a seagull asserting its presence.

"This must be paradise," Daniel observed. Raising himself up on one elbow, he looked out to the horizon.

"It definitely is," Taurean replied. "I fell in love with

this island from the first week I arrived. I was dealing with the guilt that threatened to overpower me. When I was in prison, I can't remember how many times I asked God to forgive me. Twelve years later, I'm still not sure I did the right thing, but a part of me is at peace here. I did what Corey wanted me to do. I couldn't deal with him in pain."

Daniel stared at his brother and for the first time he realized what Taurean had been through. He knew about suffering, and he knew about pain, just like Taurean.

"I'm sorry, Taurean. I never realized how much your actions affected you."

"Daniel, it took me years to forgive myself. Maybe one day the guilt will go away completely. I know you feel the same way. You blame yourself for what happened that night to Lorraine. But you need to learn to trust in God again."

"It's so much easier to say it than to feel it," Daniel replied. "I know I've grown as a person. I'm more in tune with people and helping them. Making myself look like a deity is no longer important.

"To be honest, Bro, I'm amazed at the change. One of the things the past few years have taught me is that forgiveness and love are so important. I love Alana so much that I can't imagine life without her. Mason found that with Carla, Patrick and Paula found that, too. You did once and I know you can find it again. Don't throw away a second chance to find happiness and love."

"I know what you mean, but so much about this relationship scares me. It's like my relationship with Lorraine, but it's also so different. What I had with

Lorraine was gentle and controlled. With Renée I feel intense pain when I'm with her and when I'm not. My gut feels as if it's going to rip apart with my love for her. I'm so scared at times that I wonder if it's not love but just desire."

"I've seen the way you look at her, Daniel. I know the difference between love and desire. Just trust in your feelings and it'll all work itself out. What you describe sounds so much like Alana and I, and after almost five years of marriage, I still feel just like you. And to be honest, at times it scares me that I can love someone so much."

Joanne mumbled in her sleep. The brothers laughed.

"Boy, we've got it bad with this love thing," Daniel said.

"Yeah," Taurean replied. "One thing I know about us Buchanans…when we love, we really love."

There were no more words needed, there was only the sound of the rushing waves and the rustling of the leaves above. Daniel looked out to sea, the wide expanse of ocean seemed so intimidating, but there was still peace in its vastness. In the midst of the grandeur he felt insignificant, but realized that of all that existed, he'd been given the capacity to love again. Without love, he'd ceased to exist. Now that he had allowed love back into his life, he would start to experiences life again.

A single seagull squawked above, its sound a harsh cry that seemed at odds with the cool tranquility. In the distance, a solitary figure appeared, walking along the beach. He stood immediately, knowing it was Renée.

He raised his hands waving to her, but immediately put them down.

She was standing silently, her hands outstretched to the sky as if welcoming the warm sunshine. There was something in the way she stood. A proud woman. A descendant of Africans who had been brought to these shores. Her posture may have been just that, a gesture, but to him, as she stretched her hands out, she seemed to be embracing the spirit of her ancestors.

He smiled. She was his woman. The woman whom he'd claimed as his own. All he needed to do now was let her know.

Chapter 15

Renée walked along the beach, breathing in deeply the clean, fresh, tropic breeze. She could grow to love this. She'd never traveled out of the U.S., so she'd been excited to come to an island with a reputation for its beauty. The beach stretched long and empty and she wondered where they were. She noticed someone rise from the ground. Was that Taurean or Daniel? It was Daniel. The others appeared to be relaxing on the sand.

She walked slowly toward him, stopping periodically to pick a shell up from the ground. As she got nearer, her heartbeat increased until she could feel the blood rushing through her veins. Soon, she stood a short distance from him.

Even in the warm tropic breeze she shivered, her

awareness of him even more evident because of his partial nudity. He was beautiful. She had the urge to leap into his arms. Immediately she realized the craziness of her thought. Melissa, Joanne and Taurean were there—just shows how warped her mind had become. And all because of the handsome god who stood before her.

Tonight she'd make love to him. She couldn't go another night without touching him.

"You okay?" Daniel asked, a line appearing on his forehead.

"I'm fine," she said, nodding her head slightly. "I was just taking a stroll down the beach. The island is beautiful."

"And peaceful," Daniel replied.

"I never expected it to be so wonderful. The sea is crystal clear. I can't wait to take a swim, but I don't have a swimsuit. I'll have to buy one."

"I'm sure Alana has an extra one or two. Or she can take you shopping for what you want."

"I'll be sure to ask her. I hope she can take some more time off from her painting."

She turned to glance at the sleeping dad and daughters and she felt an unexpected ache of envy. She wanted what Alana and Taurean had. It didn't matter if it was a daughter or son but she wanted a child. Her own little Buchanan.

"You want to take a walk down the beach?" she asked him. She wanted to continue exploring.

"Sure. I plan on getting a car and checking out the

island in the next few days. So here may be a good place to start."

As they started down the beach, Daniel took her hand in his.

"I plan to visit some of the island's places of interest. The last time I was here, there was no time to do much of the touristy stuff. You are free to come along with me."

"Thanks, I'd love to. I can't visit the island and not see some of it. I promised Jerome I'd take photos."

"Good. As soon as the reunion events are over we can head out on our own."

"Sure."

For a while they walked on the cool silky sand. There was no need for words between them. In fact, the sound of the gentle undulating waves only served to clear their troubled minds.

Soon they stopped to watch a group of boys diving off a nearby cliff and entering the water with more awkwardness than skill. Each time one belly-flopped in the water, raucous and hearty laughter filled the air.

"I wish I could have brought Jerome with us. He would have loved it here. It's a pity that his exams were scheduled for now."

"I would have liked him to be here, too. I'm sure that Melissa would have been glad for the company."

"Oh, yeah, I'm sure she would have been delighted."

They were now standing on the top of a tiny cliff that looked out to the ocean. Daniel stood quietly. He turned to look at Renée and she could see the anticipation in his face, the knowledge that he would kiss her.

She moved toward him, knowing that to just touch him would give relief to the ache she felt inside. Daniel pulled her in his arms and lowered his head toward hers. Their lips touched. Soft, teasing, gentle. Renée felt as if she would melt with the heat coursing through her body. The kiss deepened until she tasted his sweetness and she realized how much she missed this. He was good, knowing how to use his tongue to force a deep, heavy groan from her.

Renée placed her arms around him, drawing him even closer until she could feel every ridge and muscle in his body…until she could feel the solid, thick length of his arousal. She pulled away from him at the sound of voices. She looked down the beach. It was Taurean and the girls. They were walking toward them.

"You have exactly thirty seconds to get yourself under control or someone will realize what we've been doing," she said.

"I need to think of the saddest thing possible. I wouldn't want to embarrass you."

"Renée, Renée," shouted Melissa. "We have to go back home and shower. Daddy's taking us into Bridgetown and then to the airport to see Grandmother."

"Grandmommy, Grandmommy. I love Grandmommy. She always brings me candy," shouted Joanne.

"You ready to go back to the house?" asked Taurean.

"Yes, I'm starving."

"Good, breakfast should be ready by the time we get there." They turned and headed back to the house.

Renée glanced in Daniel's direction. He nodded. Everything was under control.

Chapter 16

Thanksgiving came without much fanfare on the island. In the U.S., families would be baking and cooking up sumptuous Thanksgiving dinners and preparing to shop on Black Friday. Here, on a smaller scale, Taurean had initiated their own celebration as part of the family reunion.

Across the island, however, banners and flags of black, gold and ultramarine flew high in the air. Songs of national pride by popular artists filled the airwaves. November was the month in which the islanders celebrated their Independence Day. Tonight, therefore, his family and friends had come together to celebrate the island's independence and embrace the tradition of the Thanksgiving dinner.

Daniel looked across the room, finding peace and

comfort as he saw each member of his family. He realized how much he'd missed them. It made all that Renée had done justifiable. He'd just been stubborn and unsure. Now that he had eased the rift he'd created with his disappearance, he felt loved and cared for. Despite this, he knew that the time away from them had taught him a lot about himself. He had needed that time.

He'd never be that man again. He felt proud of the man he'd become. He'd learned to love…unconditionally.

His mother had aged in the past few years, her hair now gray and her movements slower, but she still possessed a gentle spirit, a spirit his father had never appreciated. Daniel had loved his father with an unwavering adoration and had emulated him in every aspect of his life. He had wanted to be, and had become, the kind of minister his father had been.

However, he had also come to realize that his father had not been all he had thought. It made him sad, but his own insensitivity, his rules and his ministry of fire and brimstone had been inherited from his father. He knew now that sometimes God came to people in a still, small voice.

Daniel watched as his mother reached over to touch Renée's hand, and felt a surge of happiness. Everyone liked Renée. His mother had fallen instantly for her charm. It had made the slight scolding he'd received from her a bit more manageable. His mother could not believe that he had moved back to Chicago and not called her—but she'd forgiven him. She understood that he had needed the time on his own. He'd not expected her response. He'd expected anger. Instead his mother had taken him in her arms and cried tears of joy. Later, they talked for hours, but he'd felt the intensity of her love. Again, he'd seen God working.

Daniel watched as his brother Mason strode toward him. He didn't know Mason well, since they'd only met once before Lorraine's death. Mason had always struck him as the strong, loyal, dependable type, and in the past few days he had come to realize that his first impression was correct. What did surprise him was Mason's wit and sense of humor; a welcome change since the Buchanan males were known for their brooding personalities. He still remembered that day not long ago when they had discovered they had another brother.

"What's up, Bro?" Mason asked, his amber eyes twinkling with amusement.

"Just thinking," he replied.

"So that's the reason for the serious, brooding look? Lighten up, Dan. It's Thanksgiving, and Christmas is just around the corner."

"I know. But I'm cool. Just thinking how fortunate I am. I have so many people who care about me. I love my family and it feels good to know I'm important to them."

"I know exactly what you mean. For me it was definitely a bit more than just that. You're happy and content with your life and one morning you wake up and realize that everything you knew could be changed by one single thing. I'm sure you felt that way."

"It must have been difficult to deal with a new family, especially this big one."

"It was a bit at first, but when I met Taurean I knew

things would be all right. He made me feel a part of everything. He didn't blame me for something I had no control over. Ironically, I'm now the big brother, but I feel as if he's the more mature one," Mason said.

"Taurean has not had life easy. Those years in prison took their toll. We've all had to deal with issues in our lives. I dealt with mine in a more radical way. But I know I've been changed by the experience, and for the better. You wouldn't have liked the person I was if you'd really met me three years ago."

"No, I can't imagine you being any different," Mason commented.

"Oh, I assure you I was," Daniel said. "You know the expression 'Pride comes before a fall.' Well, that was me, and when I fell, I fell hard."

"Then the fall must have been worth it. You picked yourself up and here you are. Much improved…the person you want to be."

"I wish it had been that easy, but I did pick myself up. In the past few months I've made more progress than I did in the years I alienated myself."

"Does it have anything to do with the young lady over there?" Mason asked, his gaze directly ahead.

Daniel's eyes followed the line of Mason's vision, but even before he saw her, he knew who his brother meant, and the tingle of awareness began at his nape of his neck.

As expected, she stood with Alana, her back turned away from him. For some reason, he felt she'd been avoiding him. Since that first night in his bed she had not returned. During the day they would meet and chat briefly, but they would hardly talk, as if somehow talking would reveal feelings they did not want to deal with. Renée had thrown herself into the excitement of the planning for the Thanksgiving dinner, so Daniel had a hard time catching her without the other ladies in the kitchen. But tonight all the planning would come to an end and she'd have no excuse to avoid him. He had to make sure he spent some time with her. In a few days he planned on touring the island. With only one more week to go, they'd soon be heading back home.

Renée turned as if she sensed his eyes on her. Across the room, their eyes connected. Renée smiled, nodding at him. Even now he could feel the tension between them. He ached for her. It had been too long since he had made love to her and his need for her was so powerful he wasn't sure what he'd do.

"Um, Bro, if you don't control yourself, you're going to go over and make love to her right there on the floor." Mason chuckled.

"Okay, I admit it. I didn't know it was possible to want someone so much," Daniel responded, a hint of amusement in his voice. There was no sense in denying his feelings.

"I know exactly what you mean, Daniel. You see Carla. It's been more than two years since we got married and I can't get enough of her. I thought it would have lessened over time, but we could hop each other's bones every night. We're still like rabbits in heat."

Daniel laughed in response.

"And on that note, I have some good news I plan to share at dinner in a few minutes."

“I’m listening,” Daniel replied.

“You’ll be glad to know there’s another Buchanan on its way.”

“Mason, that’s great news!” Daniel said, thumping his brother on the back. “How far along?”

“Carla is at two months. We just discovered the day before we left for Barbados, so I’m still giddy with excitement. I’m not getting any younger, and I really don’t want to be running around with small children when I should be a granddad. I think we’ll be settling for just one. Plus I’m sure there’ll be a few more cousins before long. The Buchanan brothers seem to be quite fruitful in their old age.”

They laughed. The sound of Alana speaking up interrupted their conversation.

“Ladies and gentlemen, Thanksgiving dinner is ready,” Alana announced. “Let’s all go into the dining room.”

“I could eat a cow,” Mason said, already walking in the direction the other family members had taken.

“Mason, need I remind you that this is Thanksgiving. No cow. Just turkey!”

They laughed, a loud trumpeting sound that echoed throughout the room. Heads turned in their direction, but nobody cared. It was Thanksgiving. They were all happy.

Daniel walked along the beach, sand between his toes. He’d eaten his fill, until his stomach felt as if it would burst.

The others had retired to bed, but he needed to walk

things off. He couldn't sleep. His body felt alive and restless with his need for Renée. Heat coursed through him despite the slight chill of the night breeze.

It must be midnight. He'd always loved this time of day. When he'd been a minister, he had written most of his sermons at this time of night. He had also spent hours upon hours on his knees in prayer at the late hour. To him, midnight was the time of day when it was most peaceful, when all the worries and cares of the day could just be released into the vast unknown and be forgotten. It was the time he felt most free.

A sound behind him broke the silence and he turned quickly around.

A shadow moved toward him.

Renée.

Even in the dull light from the moon, he could tell it was her. The size of her delicate frame, the way she walked, it just was her.

"Renée?"

"Yes," she replied. He could see her face now and what he saw was a reflection of what he knew burned in his own eyes.

"What are you doing here?" he asked rhetorically. He knew exactly why she was there.

She moved closer to him, only stopping when her body touched his and her breasts rested against his chest. Daniel moved even closer until their bodies melted into each other and they were one.

Daniel lowered his head until his lips hovered above hers.

"I want you, Renée Walker. I want you so bad I can't sleep."

"I want you, too," she moaned.

Daniel ran his hand down her back, remembering the sensitive spot along her spine. She breathed in deeply, her body tense with her need.

"Come," Daniel said. "I want to make love to you right here on the sand."

They moved toward the line of tall palm trees, stopping when they reached the shadows where no one could see them.

Resting her back against one of the trees, he looked down at her, only to see her eyes were closed.

"Look at me, Renée. I want you to look at me," he said, his voice husky with desire.

She complied, her eyes bright lights in the darkness.

"I love to feel your eyes on me, knowing that you want me just as much as I want you." He lowered his head, capturing her lips in a kiss that caused his body to harden.

While he kissed her, her hands worked their magic, caressing him with a steady firmness that made him press his body onto hers. But Renée pushed him back, her fingers tugged at the buttons on his shirt, freeing them and slipping the shirt off.

Her lips broke their kiss, moving downward to his neck where she nibbled softly before moving to his chest. She placed her lips on one nipple, biting softly until he moaned with pleasure. She suckled briefly and then flicked it with her tongue.

Her lips continued their journey downward, trailing through the hair that disappeared below his jeans. Then her hand found his pants. She unzipped them, letting them fall to the sand. The cool breeze caressed his hardness, a pleasure in itself, and then her hands touched him, gliding along his thick length. Daniel tried not to scream his pleasure, but could not contain the primitive cry of lust that broke the silence.

Renée stroked him, her hand firm as his penis grew even harder with his arousal. He wanted her now. When he could bear it no more, he held her hands, placing them at her side. He bent to the ground, reaching into his pants pocket to pull out the condom he carried in his wallet. He slipped it on. He had planned to work his magic on her with his lips, but his need to be fully joined with her was stronger.

Later in bed he'd make love to her. Now, he wanted some good old-fashioned animalistic passion. Daniel placed his hands behind her back, unzipping the simple dress she wore. It slipped to the ground. His hand reached down…she wasn't wearing anything else.

His hand covered her soft down of hair. Parting it with a finger, he slipped inside her, finding her tiny nub of pleasure.

When she was ready and moist, he replaced his hand, placing his erection at her entrance.

"I want you inside me now, Daniel. Please," she pleaded, her voice heavy with her passion.

Daniel thrust inside her and she cried out in ecstasy. He paused briefly.

"Don't stop," she responded, her hand gripping his buttocks.

So he moved, a straight thrust backward and forward, backward and forward, in and out. He stroked her firmly. He stroked her hard.

Then he changed his movement, circling his hips until he could feel the head of his penis touch the very walls of her vagina. The sensation was as sweet as the island's sugar cane juice and thick, tart molasses. He continued to thrust deeply, each stroke joining them together, each stroke bringing them closer to the place of ultimate pleasure.

And then her womanhood gripped him even tighter with each stroke, clutching him until he could feel every contraction of her muscles.

"This feels so good," he cried. "It feels so damn good. I could die doing this and I would think I'm in heaven."

And then it happened…the beginning of the end. His body tensed and he knew release would come. His body was on fire, the heat coursing through every vein. Daniel increased his speed, willing the explosion, which would give him ultimate joy.

His penis tightened and contracted and his legs began to weaken. He trembled uncontrollably, unable to stop his reaction. He stretched his arms out, gripping a tree to maintain his balance and then he felt the sweet pain of release. Wave after wave of energy washed over him, causing his body to jerk as spasm after spasm contracted his body.

Then Renée's own reaction kicked in. She gripped

him tightly, as she, too, gave in to the sweetness that surged through her body. Seconds later she collapsed against him, breathing deeply, and he held on to her, his own body weak with the power of his orgasm.

For what seemed like hours they continued to hold each other, knowing that what had taken place was something powerful and special. But no one spoke the words.

When he did move, he searched for his pants on the sand and when he found them, placed them on a log that lay nearby. He pulled her onto his lap, her nakedness smooth against his hard body.

Minutes later, he said. "Come, we should probably get back to the house. I hope we haven't given anyone a show already."

They dressed quickly and walked back up the beach.

Daniel knew that the night had not ended yet. He wanted her again already, and knew that before sunrise he'd be making love to her once more.

Renée glanced at Daniel one more time, the love inside swelling until it started to hurt. She loved him. She loved this man who'd had to deal with so much in his life. She loved this man who was generous, loving, sensitive and at times so unsure of his place in this world. But he was growing stronger each day.

She smiled. They'd made love a second time that night. This time, he'd made love to her gently, like taking a stroll along the beach on a starlit night. She'd known then that she wanted to spend the rest of her life with him.

She opened the door and closed it behind her. She had to get out of there. If she didn't, she would find herself waking him, wanting him to make love to her yet again. Her insatiable appetite surprised her. She'd never been like this before. This time she seemed to have lost all control. She was practically convinced that he had her under some magic spell.

Downstairs, she headed for the kitchen where breakfast was always served. When she entered, Taurean was the only one there.

He looked up, smiling at her. "Good morning," he said, in his usual cheerful manner.

"Good morning. Are we the only ones up?" she asked.

"Yes, everyone seems to be exhausted after the long day and night. Go fill your plate and come chat with me. I'm glad for the company. Melissa is usually up to have breakfast before I head over to the resort, but when I peeked in on her she was still in dreamland."

She headed over to the breakfast table and placed some cereal in a bowl. A plate filled with local "bakes" and "fishcakes" completed the meal. Being on the island had given her a hearty appetite and she suspected she would be a few pounds heavier by the time she returned to Chicago.

She sat and started to eat, savoring the exotic but delicious taste of the local fare. They ate in silence, but there was a comfortable camaraderie that continued to surprise her. She felt safe around the Buchanan men.

Ten minutes later, she placed her fork on the plate, and sighed with satisfaction.

"It's good to see a woman who can enjoy a meal. No birdlike portions for you," Taurean said quietly, placing his own fork on his plate.

"I'm sure you are, but I pay lots at the gym to make sure I keep the pounds off. Cardio work three times a week and some light weights do the job," she replied, reaching for a handful of grapes from the basket in the center of the table. "I see you work out, too."

"I do. Remnants of prison," he said. For a moment she saw a haunted look in his eyes, but he quickly recovered. "I started working out here. I have a personal gym here—feel free to use it when you want. You won't have to work out so hard when you get back to Chicago."

"I'll be sure to," she replied.

"So you live in Chicago and work at the hospital there?" he asked.

"Yes, I've been at the hospital for the past few years. As soon as I finished my M.A. in Social Work I applied for the position and was lucky to get it."

"You must enjoy working with people?"

"Yes, I do. I've always loved working with people. You'd be surprised at the number of people who come to the hospital who have serious problems that have to be dealt with."

"You met Daniel there?"

"Yes, he wasn't a patient, though. In fact, he'd actually just saved a young girl from being beaten by her pimp."

"And Daniel came into your life," he commented.

"Yes, I saw this big, troubled man. He looked so sad. I felt sorry for him and wondered what could have caused such sadness. In the meantime, I was falling in love with him. I tried to convince myself otherwise. So I made a vow. I'd connect with him and see what I could do to help him to heal. I had no intention of becoming further involved with him. I saw a wounded man and wanted to help. That's the reason I made friends with him."

There was a sound at the door and they turned suddenly.

Daniel stood there, his face carrying a look of hurt and disappointment. With a look that sent daggers through her body, he turned and walked away.

The first thing to cross Renée's mind was what she'd just said. *I saw a wounded man and wanted to help him. That's the reason I made friends with him.* He'd heard her words.

"Go to him, Renée. Don't let him run away without hearing your explanation," Taurean said.

She left the room immediately, racing upstairs to see if he was in his room. He wasn't there. Back downstairs she headed for the beach. She suspected he'd go there. She raced down the rocky pathway until she landed on the soft cold sand.

In the distance she saw him. He stood at the far end of the beach where they'd made love the night before. She wondered how he'd gotten there so quickly.

She walked slowly, wondering if he would ever forgive her. But there was a part of her that was angry and upset, as well. How could he believe, after all they'd shared, that she didn't care?

A short distance from him she stopped and hesitated. Should she go to him? Could she love a man who thought the worst of her?

Daniel watched as Renée walked toward him. He wasn't sure if he wanted to talk to her. What he'd overheard gave him physical pain.

She'd felt sorry for him. Sorry for the poor, pathetic, tortured man. To her, he was just another job, another troubled individual who needed her help. Nothing more, nothing less. At the end of the year, he'd probably become a statistic in her annual report.

How could he have allowed himself to fall so easily for a woman who didn't really care about him? Who only saw him as wounded?

But something felt wrong.

Why was she here on the island with him? Did their lovemaking feel like duty? Could the passion that exploded between them be something she faked?

Was he being an idiot?

They'd shared too much. They'd loved too much.

"Daniel." She'd reached the place where he stood.

He turned to her and saw the tears in her eyes. He'd made her cry. And he knew. He knew that she loved him. He didn't know what had gone wrong, but they'd talk.

"You know that you didn't hear all of my conversation," she said.

"I guess so," he replied. "I'm being a self-righteous idiot, aren't I?"

"Yes, you are," she replied.

He stepped toward her, stopping when he was standing before her. He looked deep into her eyes, seeing something he should have seen before.

"Let me explain," she said, taking his hands. "I told Taurean that I fell in love with you and I was scared. I convinced myself that I would only become friends with you, so that I could help you. I did do that at first, but it was because I was terrified of falling in love, but I'd already fallen. I think I fell in love with you the night I met you, the night you saved Jamie."

He placed his arms around her, holding her closely as if he didn't want to let her go.

"I knew I was wrong. After what we shared last night, I would be crazy to question what we have. I'm sorry," he said, kissing her on the top of her head. "Forgive me?" he asked.

"Of course, Daniel. How can I not forgive you? You haven't even done anything wrong. It was just a simple misunderstanding."

"Okay. Good. So I also think I heard you say that you love me, Ms. Walker?"

"No question about it, Mr. Buchanan."

"So what do you say about us getting married?"

"Maybe if you ask me in a more romantic way." She smiled.

Daniel laughed. He bowed and prostrated himself on the ground, one knee bent.

"My darling Renée, I have loved you since the very

first moment you practically chased me out of the hospital. Would you give me the honor of being your husband?"

"Absolutely." Renée beamed. "But there are two conditions."

"And what are those?"

"That we don't have a long engagement."

"That sounds good to me. And the other one?"

"That we have at least one more child?"

"One *more?*"

"Daniel, don't forget Jerome. We already have a son."

He laughed loudly, a sound the echoed along the beach.

"Yes, we do have a son already, don't we?"

"Yes, we already have a family."

He pulled her close and hugged her tightly.

"I love you, Renée Walker," he said, his lips finding hers.

Overhead, a flock of blackbirds squawked their approval.

Epilogue

Renée woke to silence. She glanced at the empty space next to her. Daniel was not there.

She glanced at the clock. It was just after midnight.

She slipped from under the covers, stepped out of bed and headed for the balcony.

Her husband stood there, his nearly naked body magnificent under the golden glow of the moonlight.

"Daniel, suppose our neighbors see you out here like that."

"I'm sure that the old granny next door wouldn't mind an eyeful."

She giggled and slipped her arms around him. Immediately his manhood stirred.

"What are you doing out here at this time?" she asked, but she already knew the answer.

"Just thinking."

She didn't ask, but knew he'd tell her. He always did.

"About this. You, our son, our family," he eventually said. "Today is Thanksgiving and I have so much to thank God for. I know you're happy to have the whole family here, especially Jamie. I'm glad she decided to go back to school. I'm so happy that she loves living at Gloria's and has adjusted so well."

"We do have much to be thankful for. And me, I have the greatest man in the world and a wonderful son. I don't need anything else. Except…"

"Except what?" Daniel asked, a knowing look on his face.

"Want to go work on those babies we finally decided we wanted?" she said, smiling seductively.

"I've been wondering when you'd ask."

She tiptoed closer and placed her lips on his.

Above, the midnight moon smiled down on them, basking them in its warm glow.

Midnight.

The perfect time for lovers.

* * * * *